David Hill

Bound by an Oath

David Hill

Bound by an Oath

ISBN/EAN: 9783337334284

Printed in Europe, USA, Canada, Australia, Japan

Cover: Foto ©Andreas Hilbeck / pixelio.de

More available books at **www.hansebooks.com**

BOUND BY AN OATH

A Domestic Drama in Four Acts and a Prologue

BY

DAVID HILL

AUTHOR OF "FORCED TO THE WAR," "OUT OF HIS SPHERE,"
"PLACER GOLD," ETC.

*First produced by the Thespian Society of Barton Landing, Vt.,
February 28, 1888*

BOSTON

Walter H. Baker & Co.

1890

CHARACTERS.

(As originally cast by "The Thespian Society.")

PHILIP RAYMOND	. *A blind miller*	. THOMAS LANDON
JACOB JOHNSON .	. *A speculator*	. N. L. STIMPSON
SETH RANDOLPH	. *A vagabond*	. D. W. HILDRETH
EDWARD LE ROY	. *In love with Mabel*	. ED. MERREL
ELIAS AMSDEN .	. *"Bound by an Oath"*	. WILL ALLEN
SAMBO . . .	. *Servant to Jacob*	. I. M. CONNER
DRUCILLA JOHNSON .	*Sister to Jacob*	MISS L. M. ROBBINS
LUCY SNUFF . .	. *A lone widow*	MRS. D. W. HILDRETH
MRS. RAYMOND .	. *Wife of Philip*	MISS MYRTIE STIMPSON
MABEL RAYMOND	. *Daughter of Philip*	MRS. H.W. BUCHANAN
OFFICER, ETC. .		

"THE THESPIAN SOCIETY" was organized in December, 1873, by Capt. S. B. Tucker. From that time until the present (1890) it has continued to flourish, and is still running with many of the original cast. No other country Dramatic Society, I think, can be found that has held together for this number of years, or that has received so many comments from the press in its own as well as other States. In 1887, D. W. Hildreth (David Hill) took charge of the club, and presented his new play, "Forced to the War," which was received with phenomenal success. This induced him to try his hand at another production, and in 1888, "Bound by an Oath" was presented with like, if not better, results. The members most worthy of mention in making this club a success are S. B. Tucker, C. H. Colley, H. W. and E. M. Buchanan, N. L. Stimpson, C. Ford and wife, E. Merrel, T. Landon, Miss C. Parker, Miss L. M. Robbins, Miss May Johnson, Miss L. Rogers, and Mrs. H. W. Buchanan, not to mention your humble servant and wife. D. W. HILDRETH.

PROPERTIES.

PROLOGUE. — Gun cotton, for lightning. Knives, revolvers and torch for light.

ACT 1. — SCENE 1. Table, chairs, sofa, books, pen, ink, paper, cabinet, etc., etc. Large hanging mirror, R. C. Knife and revolvers for Seth. Tumbler, bottle, tray, etc. — SCENE 2. Bundles for Lucy, and letter for Sambo. — SCENE 3. Wheelbarrow, bundles, rustic chair, letter, Bible, small bundle, etc.

ACT 2. — SCENE 1. A cot, stand, stool and candle for each room. Tumbler, pipe, small box, wallet, false money, long wallet, and dark lantern. — SCENE 2. Bundles, box containing old glass arranged to break down. — SCENE 3. Same as in Act 1 ; also fan, packages of false money, large book, notes, etc.

ACT 3. — SCENE 1. Same as in Act 1, Scene 1. Also letter, revolver and phial. — SCENE 2. Bible and cane for Phillip. — SCENE 3. Table, chairs, etc. Furniture plain. Gun cotton, cup and saucer, large candle, letter, etc. — SCENE 4. — Gun cotton, zinc for thunder, rain box, wind, smoke pots, red lights, candles, phial, wallets, paper-knife, revolvers, pan of coal, check, bottle and tumbler.

ACT 4. — SCENE 1. Shawl, sunbonnet, Bible, etc. — SCENE 2. Wallet and paper. — SCENE 3. Phial, knife, revolver, handcuffs, etc.

COSTUMES MODERN AND APPROPRIATE.

DESCRIPTION OF FIRE SCENE (Act 3, scene 5). Take three blocks eight inches square, and bore six holes in each block an inch in diameter, and two inches deep. Fill these holes with red fire, placing a fuse in each for quick lighting. Place one directly under trap, one outside of room occupied by Seth, and the other outside of room occupied by Elias. Then take three iron plates (spiders with handles attached will be found the most convenient) and after saturating a quantity of wicking with turpentine mixed with resin, cover each plate with a small amount, and place with red fire. Keep a quantity near at hand to feed fire if it should diminish. If help is scarce, the work can be accomplished in the following manner: When Jacob starts to fire the mill, he does so by lighting the red fire, one tub at a time as needed, and also the wicking, both of which are directly under Seth's window outside. Edward, who is beneath the trap, cautiously removes a board, previously arranged in the floor of room occupied by Seth, and lights wicking underneath. This causes flames and a dense smoke to pour into the room. This smoke has an agreeable odor, and can be inhaled without choking or any dire effects whatever, and is perfectly safe. Just before Seth enters trap, Edward lights red fire beneath it and hastens out by a back exit. When Seth lifts trap door, which same must lift toward audience, the red light and fire is distinctly seen and into which he descends. He then controls this part of the fire himself. The fire outside of the room occupied by Elias is run the same way. Care must be taken to not let the lights diminish until scene closes. I have worked this scene several times as described, and find it can be easily done, and with little expense. The mill scene is also simple. Tuck cotton cloth upon frames for the sides, back and centre, and paint it a dirty yellow, excepting two feet and a half which is painted to represent sheathing. Wall paper can be used if necessary. In Seth's room, window should be back, and door L. C. In room occupied by Elias, door should be back, and small window R. C. Centre scene should contain a square aperture closed up with boards arranged to remove.

THE AUTHOR.

SYNOPSIS.

PROLOGUE. *Interior of cave.* The storm. Robbery and murder. Bound by an oath: "As God is my witness, I will keep this secret until my dying day." Tableau.

(*Lapse of five years between Prologue and First Act.*)

ACT I.

SCENE I. *Parlor in Johnson's house.* Surrounded by wealth. Sambo in trouble. Return of Seth Randolph. A murder prevented by a mirror. Drucilla's courage. "Rats." Seth runs the establishment.

SCENE II. *Highway.* Interview between Sambo and Lucy. "Hev you got the valerian cremens, or are you clean gone crazy."

SCENE III. *Yard in front of Raymond's house.* The blind miller and his family. Jacob Johnson again. His demand for the hand of Mabel. The refusal. Jacob's threat. The blind miller's opinion of Jacob. "It ain't for me to murmur agin the Lord — it ain't my way; but when he put that theer man together He made a great mistake." Edward and Mabel. Elias the oath-bound. Face to face. "For God's sake, who are you?" "Elias Amsden, the lad ye bound by an oath."

ACT. II.

SCENE I. *Interior of mill.* Elias and Edward. The hidden money. Elias and his secret. "O money! money! you are the bane of my life; but I worship you as a God!"

SCENE II. *Highway.* Sambo and Lucy again. "Lor a-mighty! who crushed de tea-set? who broke down de box? Who de — " A ludicrous scene.

SCENE III. *Room in Johnson's house.* Jacob and Drucilla. The wolf and the lamb. Mabel pleads for her parents. Jacob's demand. Seth interferes. Edward and Elias. They pay Raymond's notes. Jacob's discovery. "Every dollar of that money is a base counterfeit." Edward and Elias charged with counterfeiting. Deeper in the toils than ever. Seth Randolph's remorse. Elias driven to despair. "Oh, I be doomed — doomed."

ACT III.

SCENE I. *Parlor in Johnson's house.* Two rogues well met. Plan to secure Mabel. Seth refuses to act. Face to face with Elias. His curse. Jacob's villainy. Plan to drug Seth Randolph and Elias, and burn them together with the mill. A diabolical plot.

SCENE II. *Highway.* Turned into the streets. Phillip's trust in the Lord. "He will guide us through the wilderness like as he did the Israelites of old, if we're not afeer'd to trust Him." Discovered by Lucy. A friend in need. "Now you just follow me and I'll take you home in a half a jiffy."

SCENE III. *Room in Lucy's house.* Mabel and the letter. The hound still upon the track. Mother and daughter. "Then, though I crush my heart in doing it, I will marry Jacob Johnson."

SCENE IV. *Highway.* Jacob started to burn the mill.

SCENE V. *Interior of mill.* Edward and Elias. Edward in hiding. Elias contemplates suicide in order to reveal the oath. Seth and Jacob. The check. The drugged wine. Seth outwitted. "Oh, I am lost! lost!" Jacob fires the mill. Storm, flames and smoke. Seth recovers. Locked in. To the rescue of Elias. Edward beneath the trap. A double rescue. Seth Randolph saved but dying. "Let — let me speak! Ja — Jacob — O God! — he — Jacob — he done this — he —"

ACT IV.

SCENE I. *Room in Lucy's house.* Mabel and Lucy. Phillip's anxiety. Learns of Mabel's object. Off to the rescue. "Lead the way, Betty, and I'll follow you with the strength of a giant."

SCENE II. *A wood.* Confession and death of Seth Randolph. "Place me where the birds can sing over me and where streaks of sunshine can reach my grave."

SCENE III. *Parlor in Jacob's house.* Drucilla and Jacob. She criticises his actions. "Mr. Johnson, outside from bombast and cynicism, you are of little account." The dove in the eagle's claw. Elias to the rescue. Phillip, Mrs. Raymond and Lucy. Elias attempts suicide. Timely arrival of Edward. "Kill the fatted calf, the prodigal has returned." Jacob in the toils. Return of the money. A happy termination.

BOUND BY AN OATH.

PROLOGUE.

SCENE. — *Interior of cave. Dark stage. Lightning and thunder, with wind and rain. As curtain rises,* ELIAS AMSDEN *rushes in from* R. I E.

ELIAS. There! now I be safe from the storm. Swift as I was it nearly overtook me before I reached the cave. How dark it grows! And the wind, how it moans! (*Lightning and heavy thunder.*) Heavens! what a flash! That must ha' struck somewheres. Outside the cave is a big hemlock — (*Goes to mouth of cave and looks off* R. I E.) Mercy! it's all ablaze. How quickly the lightning set it on fire. (*Lightning and thunder.*) There goes another flash! (*Retreating back into cave.*) It be safer in here, though I ha' no love for the darkness. (*Cries of "Help! help!" heard off* R. I E.) Hark! what was that? Did I not hear cries for help? (*Cries repeated.*) There it is again. (*Goes to mouth of cave and looks off* R. I E.) Oh, Heavens! there be two men bearing the body of another between them. They be passing the burning hemlock. Why, they be coming this way. (*Running back into cave.*) Oh, what shall I do! If I be seen I shall surely share the same fate. (*Noise outside.*) They be close at hand. I will hide if there be a place to put me. (*Goes down cave* C. L., *and hides behind big boulder. Storm dies away as scene progresses.*)

(JACOB JOHNSON *and* SETH RANDOLPH *enter* R. I E., *with the body of their victim. They deposit body near center of stage.*)

SETH. Hark'ee, now, Jacob, I'm a second Pilate. I wash my hands of this murder. Understand?

JACOB. You do — eh? Wash your hands of a murder which you helped to commit. Slip your own neck out of the noose, and leave me to hang. Help get me into the trap, and then desert me because I happened to strike the blow.

SETH. Yes, yes, Jacob; but you struck too hard — altogether too hard. Murder was not my intention. We wanted the money — that was natural. To secure it, it

5

necessitated a blow; but that blow should have been given gently — gently, Jacob. Indeed! so gently, that the spark of life would have remained. You overdid the job, Jacob.

JACOB. Well, it's done, and can't be undone. I struck too hard, I admit that, but he should not have struggled. He aggravated the assault through his own desperate endeavor to escape. Had he yielded to our demand, no trouble would have ensued. However, now that the deed is done, what are you going to do about it?   .

SETH. I don't know, Jacob. On that point my heart is exceptionally tender. I long for his resuscitation. Bring him to life, Jacob, and I'll return my half of the boodle without a struggle.

JACOB. Bah! this accident has frightened you. It has made you tender and chicken-hearted as a woman; and women are cowards.

SETH. Not always, Jacob. The most heroic act I ever witnessed was performed by a woman. That act was the saving of my miserable carcass from a watery grave. Indeed! she rescued me from a position so perilous, that even men shuddered to make the attempt. Don't stigmatize a woman, Jacob, because if you do, what little sense of manhood I have left will rebel in an instant.

JACOB (*after a pause*). Well!

SETH. Well, Jacob.

JACOB. Something must be done.

SETH. There must! I admit that.

JACOB. What shall it be?

SETH (*advancing front*). I pass; you can play it alone.

JACOB (*following and tapping him on shoulder*). Seth, come back. (*They go down stage.* SETH, L., JACOB, R.) This is no place to show the white feather. The deed is done, and you must help cover it up. This cave is rarely if ever visited. The stranger whom we have disposed of is unknown in these parts, and will never be missed. I have a few suggestions to make.

SETH. Make them.

JACOB. Let us bury the body, divide the money, swear eternal secrecy to each other, and part for ever.

SETH. Your suggestions are adopted, especially the latter. To one, however, I object.

JACOB. What is that?

SETH. Dividing the money. I want none of it. My conscience is against it.

JACOB. You are a coward.

SETH (*turning upon him fiercely*). You lie.

JACOB (*touching revolver*). What!

SETH. I mean, in the present sense of the word. I am a coward only as a guilty conscience makes me one. No matter how much I craved that money under ordinary circumstances, it has no charms for me when bathed in human blood. You struck the blow, and have earned the reward. I won't touch it.

JACOB. Well, will you help to bury the body?

SETH. I suppose I must.

JACOB. Then search with me for a fagot. We need a light. (*They search for fagot.*)

SETH (*finding fagot*). Here is your fagot — light it. (JACOB *lights it.*)

JACOB. Now for an examination of the cave. (*Goes down stage followed by* SETH.) The Devil could not have chosen a better place.

SETH (*sarcastically*). Or better subjects for it, eh, Jacob?

JACOB. Silence! your remarks are too pointed. Here! look at this boulder. It juts out over, leaving a large cavity underneath. Stow the body in there, and only the resurrection can find it. (*Discovers* ELIAS, *and jumps back in surprise.*) The Devil!

SETH (*starting*). Eh — what! have you found him already?

JACOB. The Devil? No; would that I had. (*Dragging* ELIAS *from behind rock.*) How came you here?

SETH. I should remark the same.

ELIAS. I was sheltering myself from the storm. I saw you coming, and so concealed myself.

JACOB. Have you overheard our conversation?

ELIAS. I have, sir; but I could not help it — indeed I could not.

JACOB. Do you know who we are?

ELIAS. I do, sir; but I be not t' blame for that. I be not t' blame for knowing you, sir.

JACOB. Here, remain where you are. Move, and your life shall pay the forfeit. Seth?

SETH. Jacob!

JACOB. Follow me. (*They advance to front of stage.*)
We are discovered — ruined.

SETH. We are, Jacob.

JACOB. What is to be done?

SETH (*slowly*). Hang!

JACOB (*starting*). Hang? Not while this right arm can
strike. The sod that covers one can cover two ; and a dead
tongue is ever silent. He must die.

SETH. Must?

JACOB. So I remarked. To avoid any disagreement
between ourselves, we will settle the question by tossing a
coin. Whoever the choice falls upon, must dispose of the
boy. Do you consent?-

SETH (*after a pause*). I consent.

JACOB (*taking coin from his pocket*). Well, here goes.
(*Tossing coin into the air.*) Name your choice.

SETH. Heads you win.

JACOB (*holds torch and looks at coin*). It is heads. You
are the boy's executioner. Perform your duty. (*Goes up
R. I E.*)

SETH. Very well. (SETH *looks toward boy, then turns,
and goes down* L. I E. *Pauses a moment, then takes long
dirk knife from his pocket and feels the edge. At last he
turns and goes down center to* ELIAS. *Slow music.*) Boy,
you see the exit to this cave? To the left is a path that
leads to your father's cottage. Take it, and go home.

JACOB (*springing down front*). What !

SETH. Jacob, stand back. This boy is in my hands — I
shall dispose of him.

JACOB. Yes, but you would set him free. Once free,
and you know the consequences.

SETH. I'll take the consequences. Though the gallows
stared me in the face, and the rope was already around my
neck, I would not harm a hair of that boy's head to save my
life.

JACOB. Are you determined?

SETH (*going down* C. L.). I am adamant.

JACOB (*going* R. I E. ; *aside*). No power can move him
when once he has decided. Something must be done, and
quickly, too. (*Aloud.*) Seth?

SETH. Jacob!

JACOB. Come here.

SETH (*to* ELIAS). Boy, don't move from your tracks until I return. (*Advances front.*) Well?

JACOB. If you refuse to dispose of him, you must frighten him into silence. I have known him from an infant. When once his word is given he is as immovable as yourself. Extort from him a promise to keep this a secret, and jve are safe; otherwise, you know the consequences. Are you for, or against it?

SETH. I am for it, Jacob, just so long as it don't take blood. If it comes to that, I enter a protest. You are better adapted for the frightening process than I am, so I surrender the case into your hands. Do it gently, though, as gently as possible without resorting to force.

JACOB. Leave that to me. (JACOB *goes down* R. *with torch.* SETH *turns* L.)

SETH. Boy, I have changed my mind. Unless you swear eternal secrecy in this matter, — well, you've got to go under, that's all. You had better swear. This man will do the business, I can't.

ELIAS (*clinging to* SETH). Oh, no — no! For the love of Heaven, let me live! Oh, I beg of you not t' murder me!

JACOB. Shut up! (SETH *pushes him over to* JACOB.) Another word, and it's all over with you. Now listen. Our conversation must have convinced you that this murder was unintentional. The law, however, knows no difference. Swear upon your sacred honor to keep it a secret, and you are safe. Refuse, and your body shall rot in the same hole as the one beside you. Down and swear.

ELIAS (*kneeling back of corpse*). I swear it.

JACOB (*stands* R. *with revolver pointed at* ELIAS, SETH *stands* L. *the same*). Then say, "As God is my witness, I will keep this secret until my dying day."

ELIAS (*lifting his hands to Heaven*). As God is my witness, I will keep this secret until my dying day.

JACOB. You swear it?

ELIAS. I swear it. (*Tableau.*)

JACOB.	ELIAS.	SETH.
	CORPSE.	

Lapse of five years between Prologue and first Act.

ACT I.

SCENE I. — *Parlor in* JOHNSON'S *house. Folding doors back looking into room beyond. Table with books, etc.,* L. I E. *Side entrances* L. *and* R. *Lounge* C.L. *Large hanging mirror* C. R. *Secretary* L. *Altogether, a richly furnished apartment. As curtain rises,* JACOB *and* DRUCILLA *enter from* R. 3 E. JACOB *comes down* L. DRUCILLA, R.

JACOB (*impatiently*). Come, come, Drucilla, you've harped on that long enough. The girl suits me, and if I can win her hand it's a privilege I have. Besides, this house has been without a mistress long enough.

DRUCILLA (*with toss of head*). Indeed! without a mistress. Is this my recompense for all these years of toil and drudgery? Are you aware, Mr. Johnson, that I am mistress here?

JACOB. Yes, you are mistress here, that is evident. But recollect, Drucilla, you are only a sister. As such, you cannot expect to supply the place of a loving and devoted wife.

DRU. A loving and devoted fiddlestick! What does a man at your time of life want of a wife, I wonder. Besides, the girl don't love you, and never will. If she does, she's a downright fool, that's all.

JACOB. That is, in your estimation. Remember, though, that your way of thinking is as different from mine as black is from white. You have no affection for anything, unless I except the love for darning a stocking, or sewing on a patch, which, I believe, you are especially fond of. (DRUCILLA *shrugs her shoulders.*) This girl may not love me now, but she will after marriage; at least, I will take the chances.

DRU. Well, I declare! One would think to hear you talk that the girl was already at your command. What does Mabel want of you? Are you aware that she is already in love with Edward? What are you, with your sour visage, and ungainly figure, compared with him? If I'm any judge of character, your proposition will meet with a prompt refusal; and it ought to.

JACOB. Not so fast, Drucilla. You do not consider that I hold the family within my power, and she dare not refuse.

I could turn them into the street if I desired; and as for Phillip, her father, you know the hold I have upon him?

DRU. Yes, I do; and if you take advantage of it, you are a greater rascal than I take you to be, and goodness knows you are enough of one already. However, have your own way. You always would be headstrong and unreasonable, and I expect you will in this. Remember, though, I will tolerate no undue extravagance. I won't stand it. (*Exit* R. C. D.)

JACOB (*coming down* C.). Ha! ha! ha! how little she knows of the rod I hold over the Raymond family. Every dollar they possess, the honor of the family even, is in my hands, and it rests with me to save them from poverty and disgrace. The old man is blind and helpless. The forgery that was committed, and for which he mortgaged me his place, I still hold against him; and though he was innocent, it is impossible for him to prove it. (SAMBO *enters unperceived*, C.) Before I yield up that girl, I will foreclose on the mortgage, turn the whole family into the street — aye! and place Phillip Raymond in a prison cell. Such is my vindictiveness towards those who work against me.

SAMBO. Mas'r Johnson?

JACOB (*turning quickly*). How now, you black rascal! How dare you intrude upon me thus unceremoniously!

SAMBO. 'Spects I have 'casion, Mas'r Johnson.

JACOB. What do you want?

SAMBO. I'se gwine to tole you, sah, gwine to squatulate dis yer minute. Lor a mighty! Mas'r Johnson, what you tink? Dar's a man outside what says he's a gwine to enter dis yer tickler compartment spite of de debbil sure. He tole me so with his own mouf, sah.

JACOB. He told you so, did he? What does he look like?

SAMBO. Dass it, Mas'r Johnson, dat's de tickler question I was tinking on. 'Pears to me, if I disremember perzactly, he was a resemblance to de scare-crow in Mas'r Wottle's corn field, sah.

JACOB. A beggar — eh? Tell him to be off with himself. I have no patience with any such trash.

SAMBO (*going*). Yes, sah, I'se gone, sah. (*Stops.*)

JACOB. Well, why don't you go?

SAMBO. I was tinking dat de genl'man might refuse to go, sah.

JACOB. Well?

SAMBO. Under de circumstances, de situation would be werry disembarrassing, sah.

JACOB. You are a coward. Tell him to begone, or I will order his arrest. That will settle the question at once.

SAMBO. And if he don't go den, sah?

JACOB. Clear out and do as I command you.

SAMBO. I'se gone, sah. (*Exit* C. D.)

JACOB. That negro is a regular nuisance. (*Seats himself at the table and writes.*) I will write to this Raymond family stating that I shall call upon them at two o'clock sharp. I may as well decide my fate first as last. That the girl will refuse my hand, I haven't a doubt; but the knowledge of her father's affairs will soon bring her to terms. After that I shall have nothing to fear. (*Commotion outside.*) Just as I expected! That negro's cowardice has got him into trouble. (*Rising from table.*)

SAMBO (*without*). Lor a mighty! don't shoot! don't shoot, sah! Ise not prepared to die — indeed! I isn't, sah. (*Backing in* C. D., *followed by* SETH RANDOLPH, *with pointed revolver.* SAMBO *runs behind* JACOB, *who advances front.*) O Mas'r Johnson! for de love of de Lord, save me — save me, Mas'r Johnson.

JACOB. Shut up! you black imp. (*Turning to* SETH.) Well, sir, by what authority do you enter here?

SETH (R. *of* C.). Oh, I was only trying to look Erebus out of countenance. I trust the endeavor has not occasioned you any displeasure?

JACOB. Villain! you are insolent. Leave the room, or I shall be under the necessity of resorting to force.

SAMBO (*behind* JOHNSON). Dar's gwine to be a murder in dis yer house sure's you're born.

JACOB. Are you going, sir?

SETH. Oh, not just at present. A call that is too short is as unpolished as a call that is too long. Custom has taught me to adhere strictly to etiquette. The rules of etiquette must govern my departure. (*Passing down* R. H. *corner.*)

JACOB. Your audacity is without precedent. Sambo, show him out of the house.

SAMBO (*retreating down* L. H. *corner*). O Mas'r Johnson!

JACOB. Do as I command you.

SAMBO. I couldn't do it, Mas'r Johnson. I couldn't do it nohow.

JACOB. Will you obey me, you black rascal? Why are you shivering as if stricken with the ague? Put this vagabond out of the house.

SAMBO (*shivering*). Lor a mighty! I'se dun gone for. Ise tooken wid de cranks, Mas'r Johnson. I can't move — indeed I can't, sah.

JACOB (*starting toward him*). You cowardly wretch!

SETH. Hold on there, friend! An ungovernable temper is man's worst enemy. Learn to bridle the tongue, and half of the battle is accomplished. I perceive my countenance is not familiar to you, although it is wreathed in smiles. Jacob, have you visited the old cave lately.

JACOB (*starting*). How! What!

SETH. Oh, nothing. I was merely talking as one in a dream. Look at me, Jacob. Behold in my face the old familiar land-marks of friendship. Has five years served to obliterate me from your memory?

JACOB (*looking at him sharply*). Seth Randolph!

SETH. The recognition is complete. Jacob?

JACOB. Well!

SETH. Shake. (JACOB *gives hand reluctantly*.) Jacob, do you know why I am here?

JACOB. No.

SETH. I want money.

JACOB (*starting back*). Money? Do you expect to find it here? Why, man, I haven't a dollar at my disposal.

SETH (*advancing front*). Avoid the law, and cheat the lawyer. That's my motto in rainy weather. I shall not resort to the law to get my half of this estate. Jacob?

JACOB. Well!

SETH (*pointing to Sambo*). Let Erebus pass out.

JACOB. What!

SETH. Let him pass out.

JACOB (*aside*). Curse it! I must obey him. (*Aloud.*) Sambo, you can go.

SAMBO (*starting off*). Bress de Lord! I'se jess gwine to fly.

SETH. Here you, Erebus, come back.

SAMBO (*making off*). Couldn't tink of it, sah, couldn't tink of it nohow. (SETH *points revolver at him.* SAMBO *returns.*) Lor a mighty! I'se a-coming. Put up yer popping iron, Mas'r Somebody, I'se right here.

SETH. Bring me a bottle of wine.

(SAMBO *looks at* JACOB).

JACOB. You can bring it.

SETH (*pointing off*). Go. (SAMBO *runs out* C. D.) Jacob, it has been five years since we parted with each other at the mouth of the old cave.

JACOB. Well!

SETH. Since that time my conscience has undergone a wonderful change. Indeed, so case-hardened has it become that I now demand my share of that money.

JACOB. What! would you rob me? Never! Before I will yield up that money, the law shall take its course.

SETH. And when it does it will find you upon the gallows. Kind of makes you wince now, don't it? Come; give me my share — you dare not refuse it.

JACOB. Dare not — dare not! say you? Bah! who recognizes you? What jury, after one glance at your face, would convict me on your testimony? I defy you.

SETH. Well, my face is against me, that's a fact. The face is a mirror to the heart; and when the heart is evil, the evil seems to crop out and show all over the man. However, there's the lad —

JACOB. What of him? He is demented, broken down in spirits, and no longer responsible for what he does.

SETH. And we are the cause of all this?

JACOB. Call it as you please.

SETH. Jacob, listen to me. To kill a man outright, is murder. To murder his peace of mind, is no crime. Now, to my thinking, he who ruins the happiness of another, compelling him to live in perpetual torture and mental anguish, is a greater murderer than he who robs a man of life. We are the murderers of that boy. How does it make you feel, Jacob?

JACOB. You are mad.

SETH. Mad? Then is a guilty conscience a species of insanity. Now to show you how far that insanity has taken me. (*Taking paper from his pocket.*) When I parted from

you, five years ago, I compelled you to write down every particular of that murder, and affix your signature. (*Showing
paper.*) Here is the paper — I perceive you recognize it.
Now, Jacob, unless you place five thousand dollars at my
disposal, I will hand this paper to the proper authorities, and
by so doing show up that murder to the eyes of the world.
Think it over. (*Goes up stage, and throws himself into chair
facing mirror. His back is toward audience. He leans back
in chair and lights cigar.*)

JACOB (*down* C. L. *aside*). That man must die. Until
he is disposed of I am no longer safe. Ha! a thought. His
back is toward me. I could easily steal upon him unawares,
and stab him to the heart. I then could conceal the body,
and he would never be missed. It shall be done. (*Goes
to table, opens drawer, takes out papers and dagger. He
conceals dagger; aloud.*) Seth, as you say, half of that
money belongs to you. Wait but a moment, and I will fill
out the check. (*Pretends to write check.*) There! now I
will bring it to you that you may see if it is all right. (*Conceals dagger in right hand and crosses to* SETH. *As he lifts
it to strike,* SETH, *who has watched his movements in the
mirror, suddenly points revolver at him over his shoulder.*
JACOB *starts back in surprise. Chord.*)

SETH. Jacob, stand back.

JACOB. Ha! would you murder me?

SETH. Jacob, that mirror is like your own heart; it re-
veals all there is in it.

SAMBO (*entering* C., *with wine, etc*). Here am de wine,
Mas'r Somebody.

SETH. Very well. (*Rises, takes glass, and comes down*
C. R. JACOB C. L.). Here's to your health. May you be
more successful in your next attempt. (*Drinks and returns
glass.* SAMBO *falls back.*) Jacob, fill out that check.

JACOB. Give me time. Give me a week, and you shall
have it. (*Aside.*) In that time I will dispose of him, or may
my right hand be withered.

SETH. Your wish is granted. Disappoint me, though,
and you know the consequences. Erebus, advance.

SAMBO. I'se coming, sah. (*Comes down front.*) I'se right
here, sah.

(SETH *takes glass and is about to drink as* DRUCILLA *enters*
R. 3 E.)

DRU.   Mr. Johnson, I wish to inform you — (*Perceiving* SETH.)   Why, who's this! and a glass in his hand, too. Jacob, why is such a vagabond in the house?

SETH.   Pardon me, madam; but I am your brother's most intimate and confidential friend.   Is it not so, Jacob? (*Drinks.*)

JACOB (*with difficulty*).   Ye-yes.

DRU.   I want to know! I was not aware that my brother was the associate of ruffians and beggars.   Why, his face would make a good photograph for a rogues gallery. (*Turning to* SETH.)   Do you know, sir, I take you for a contemptible worm?   Bless me! if I'm any judge of looks, you are a bold, bad man.

SETH.   Which shows, madam, how little you can read the human face.   A rough exterior often covers a costly gem. I speak that with reference to myself.   The plainer the bird, the sweeter the song.   Are — are you a vocalist, madam?

DRU.   You insulting thing! Jacob, it is my desire that this man shall leave the house.   Command Sambo to put him out.

SAMBO (*retreating down* R. C.).   O Missus! I couldn't do it! couldn't do it nohow!

DRU.   Why don't you speak, Jacob?   Has your tongue become suddenly tied?   Why do you entertain such a character in the house?

JACOB.   Drucilla, he is here —

SETH.   On particular business, madam.   Business of such a vital nature as not to require your presence.   You can go — eh, Jacob?

JACOB.   Under the circumstances, Drucilla, you had better retire.   It will only be for a short season —

SETH.   After which, you can return.   This is what the tide said to the shore: "I go; but I shall come back." And mind, no listening at the key-hole either.   A listening ear is an abomination.   Erebus, advance. (SAMBO *starts forward.*)

DRU.   Stay where you are, sir. (SAMBO *falls back.*)

SETH (*authoritatively*).   Erebus, advance. (SAMBO *starts forward again.*)

DRU. (*fiercely*).   Stay where you are, sir. (SAMBO *runs back.*)   If the master of this house is devoid of courage, I will assume command myself. As for you, you contemptible sneak — leave the house this instant.

SETH. Beautiful is woman in her natural sphere. Perverted, the Devil is no comparison. Often have I stuffed the ballot-box in their behalf, and admired them for their courage and temerity. (*Suddenly crashing tumbler upon the floor and shouting.*) Rats!!!

DRU. (*screaming and running down stage* C. R.). Mercy!

SAMBO (*jumping and dropping tray*). Lordy Gody mighty! whar is um!

SETH (*jumping into chair down* C., *and flourishing two revolvers*). Everywhere! everywhere! Cover your figurehead, you black bull of Bashan, or off goes a pendant. (SAMBO *darts under table.* DRUCILLA *holds up chair to protect herself.*) That's right! dodge about, for in it rests your safety. This house, and all there is in it, belongs to me; with the exclusive right to shoot — pop — bang — blaze away — (*Shoots revolvers around room as scene closes in.*)

(*Disposition of characters.*)

SETH (*in chair*).

SAMBO (*under table*).

DRUCILLA. JACOB.

R. L.

SCENE II. — *Highway.*

(SAMBO *enters from* L., *backing on.*)

SAMBO. Hi! dar — clar out! doan you trouble dis yer chile no mo' — doan you do it. Lor a mighty! what am de world a coming to! Tarrin' times down at Mas'r Johnson's — ebery ting discumbobalated in a heap. Nebber saw de likes in all dis yer chile's recommembrance. Dar's de Missey next ting to gone wid de steerics, and Mas'r Johnson, he doan say nuffin, but jess give me dis yer letter to deliver, an' den dat yer shooting popperer running de house. I can't see through it nohow. (*Looking off* L.) Git out, dar! doan you come dis yer way, 'cause I can't stand it! (*Enter from* R., LUCY SNUFF, *with basket and bundles. She stands and stares at* SAMBO, *who does not observe her.*) Doan want nuffin mo' to do wid yer on top of dis yer yearth. Clar out!

LUCY. What on airth is the matter?

SAMBO (*jumping back*). Hey! git out, dar—git out! I doan—(*Perceives* LUCY.) Lor a mighty! is dat you, Missey Lucy?

LUCY. Land a massey! yes. Hev you got the valerian cremens, or are you clean gone crazy. You look scater than Deacon Applejack did when the hornets chased him out of the raspberry patch. Sakes alive! didn't he run, though. Ain't anybody dead, is there?

SAMBO. Lor a mighty! dar's gwine to be a funeral at Mas'r Johnson's afore a week.

LUCY. Sakes alive! you don't say! Well, it's nuthin' more nor less than I expected. I told Drucilla last week, if she didn't wear an anica plaster atween her shoulders she'd hev the spine-on-er-gee-tus agin, spite of yarbs an' doctors. Nuthin' like an anica plaster for spine-on-er-gee-tus, I kin tell ye. When wus she tooken down?

SAMBO. Tooken down! Who? Missey Johnson? Laws a massey! dar's nuffin de trouble wid her—she nebber was took.

LUCY. I want tu know! Then Jacob is sick, is he? I knew he would be when I heard him sneeze twice afore break-fast tother mornin'. I told him then tu take a dose of cannibal innicus, an' soak his feet in hemlock tea, or he'd hev the fever worse than Uriah did, an' you know Uriah wus awful bad. He wouldn't du it, though. Men are hateful critters when they set out for it, I kin tell ye. If you ever cotch a cold, Samuel, jest take some cannibal innicus, an' soak your feet in hemlock tea. It'll help you every time. Has he hed tu hev a doctor?

SAMBO. Who! Mas'r Johnson? Dar's nuffin de trouble wid him. He doan want no doctor, Mas'r Johnson doan.

LUCY. Sho! you don't say! Then for massy's sake! who is sick?

SAMBO. Dar ain't nobody sick, I tole yer. Lor a mighty! can't dar be a funeral in de house widout de measels?

(*Crosses to* R.)

LUCY (*crossing to* L.). Well, well, goin' tu be a funeral in the house, an' nobody sick. You beat all the niggers for talkin' in columdrums I ever did see. Land a massey! I wus jest a-goin' over there; but your talk has flusterated me so, I hardly know whether tu go ahead, or jest turn around an' go back.

SAMBO. Better go back, Missey Lucy, now recommember what I tole yer. Dar's a man wid de popper irons what has taken lawful possession of de whole ting. He took it wid his own permission, he did. Doan you go near de house.

LUCY. Gracious goodness! a man taken lawful possession? Well, well, what will happen next, I wonder. (*Sets down bundles, approaches* SAMBO, *and talks significantly.*) Do you know, Samuel, I allus did think there wus somethin' kinder cur'us about Jacob's affairs? You know what the general report is, don't ye? Well, folks will talk, ye know, an' perhaps there's nuthin' tu it. Leastwise, I hope not. Then the officers have really taken possession.

SAMBO. Ossifers? Who said anything about ossifers! Dar ain't no ossifers at Mas'r Johnson's.

LUCY. Didn't you say the officers had taken possession of the house?

SAMBO. Didn't say nuffin 'bout ossifers. What fo' ossifers go to Mas'r Johnson's? He ain't stole no sheep, Mas'r Johnson ain't.

LUCY. Land a massey! who said anything about sheep! You niggers will mix things up the wust of any people I ever did see. Hev you started for anywheres in particular?

SAMBO. Wuss dat?

LUCY. I didn't know but you might be goin' down tu Phillip Raymond's. Of course I don't keer, an' only ask out of curiosity. Poor man! it wus a great caramity when his sight wus tooken from him. It does seem cur'us, though, that he should let Elias sleep in the mill, even if he does run it. Why, if it wus mine, I should know he would sot it on fire. Kind o' cur'us about that boy, now, ain't it?

SAMBO. Doan know nuffin 'bout dat Elias. Mas'r Johnson says I doan want nuffin' to do wid him.

LUCY. Massey sakes! what did he say that for? Why, there wern't no smarterer boy in town than Elias wus, afore that mystery preyed upon his mind. Why on airth he don't tell about it is mor'n I can see inter. Well, I must run along, or I shall never get there. (*Takes up basket and bundles.*) I'm goin' tu take Drucilla some corn an' cowcumbers. She's dreadful fond of cowcumbers, Drucilla is, an' then agin, she says they'er good for her dispeperie. I reckon I shant be in the way, so I'll run my chances. If you see Mrs. Raymond, you tell her my rhumatiz is a heap better, an' jest as soon as the first surveyance offers, I'll drop down an' see her. (*Starts off* L.)

SAMBO (*calling*). Missey Lucy!

LUCY (*turning back*). Well! for the land sakes what do you want now? I'm in a dreadful hurry.

SAMBO. Dar's a bran new litter of pigs down to Mas'r Wottles — see'd 'em all myself.

LUCY (*indignant*). Well, what on airth du I keer for a litter of pigs. (*Goes off* L.)

SAMBO. Ya! ya! ya! nebber saw de likes of dat ole woman on top of dis yer yearth. · Golly! she can talk faster than a guinea hen can cackle — dat's a fact. Knows eberyting, too. Lor a mighty! what she want to 'sinuate dat yer ting 'bout Mas'r Johnson fo'? 'Spects she doan know nuffin 'bout it. Ya! if I doan deliber dis yer letter mighty quick, dar'll be de debbil to pay. Mas'r Johnson'll send dat yer shooting popperer after me sure. Hi! git out dar! Doan you come dis yer way — doan you do it. (*Runs off* R.)

SCENE III. — *Yard in front of* RAYMOND'S *cottage*, R. *Porch over door entwined with vines, etc., etc. Highway leading from extreme* R. U. E., *down past cottage, and off* L. *Grist mill seen in the distance.* PHILLIP *discovered seated in rustic chair in front of cottage.* MRS. RAYMOND *stands in front of porch, with* MABEL *beside her. She holds letter in her hand as scene opens.*

MRS. R. (*reading*). "To Phillip Raymond:
                              I shall call upon you at two o'clock sharp. I particularly request that Mabel shall be present.
                              Jacob Johnson."

Alas! too well I know what that call portends; and unless his heart is unusually lenient, we shall be turned into the streets, homeless and friendless.

PHILLIP. Cheer up, Betty, cheer up. This here wureld we're living in ain't all amiss. Theer's patches of sunshine, a'most as big as the shadows, spread out all around us. I

could wish they might shine a leetle brighter sometimes —
enough to keep us and the old home together — and I reckon
they will if we don't murmur too much agin it. Don't be
down spirited, Betty, s'longs the mill wheel continues to
turn.

MRS. R. Ah, Phillip, you always look on the bright siae,
even in your sorest afflictions. Sometimes I bless Heaven
for it. But at present, our situation is most deplorable;
and unless some unforeseen event occurs, I can see nothing
but ruin staring us in the face.

PHILLIP. Well, Betty, theer's worse things than being
stared at by ruin. Now I ain't discouraged — not at present.
Them theer notes won't spile if they keeps a leetle longer.
Why! Jacob's art may have a streak of generosity run
through it; though, if he does, it will be the first in my
remembrance. Anyhow, let us sing until the lightning
strikes. Theer'll be time enough for mourning after that.

MABEL. What is his reason, think you, for wishing me
to be present?

MRS. R. Alas! my child, I know not, unless — unless —

MABEL. Why do you hesitate, dear mother?

MRS. R. Oh, I dare not speak the words that are hover-
ing on my lips! I have noticed his manner toward you of
late, and it has haunted me — filled my soul with dread. If
I am not greatly mistaken, I can too easily interpret his
meaning.

MABEL. Alas! dear mother, you do not mean —

MRS. R. I mean, my child, that Jacob Johnson cherishes
for you more than a friendly affection. What it will termi-
nate in, I dare not say; but the end is too apparent.

MABEL. O mother! you do not mean — Heaven! he
would not ask me to become his wife? Impossible! I would
rather die. I never can — I never will.

PHILLIP. And you never shall, my child, you never shall.

MRS. R. But you know, Phillip, we are completely in
his power. If he should insist upon it, what could you do?

PHILLIP. Do? Why, I'd refuse, of course. Do you
think as how another man has the power of control like a
father over his own child? The laws of God are agin it.
Blind and helpless as I am, I would beg, starve in the streets,
afore my Mabel should wed a man whom I believe —

MRS. R. (*grasping his arm*). Hush! hush! Phillip. Even now he is coming toward the house.

PHILLIP. Well, let him come. It ud do him good to hear some of the sentiments of public feeling there is agin him.

(*Enter* JACOB JOHNSON, R. U. E.)

JACOB (*touching his hat*). Ah, quite a family gathering! It delights me exceedingly to see you thus congregated together. You doubtless received my letter?

MRS. R. I have just been reading it to Phillip. We are very sorry, sir, but —

PHILLIP. Hold on, Betty, hold on right theer! What have we done to be sorry for? Not one blessed thing. (*Turning to* JACOB.) You see, sir, business have been dull lately — werry dull. The water in the stream is low, and that theer lowness keeps the grists away. If you had the art to wait a leetle longer, Jacob, just till the stream comes up — no longer, maybe — perhaps I could do something by you. I ud try it, anyhow.

JACOB. Yes, yes; no doubt your intentions are all right. Recollect, however, that your property, at forced sale, would not pay me the amount of your indebtedness. Have you made any provisions for your payments in case of a postponement?

PHILLIP. On'y the arnings of the mill. Beyond that, I can't say.

JACOB. Then you must not blame me for foreclosing on the mortgage. Well, let that rest. I am a man of few words, and will come to the point at once. I want your daughter for my wife. She has doubtless perceived before this, that I have cherished more of an affection for her, than others of her kind. My social position, my wealth, and I trust, her respect for me, will lead to an acceptance of my hand.

MABEL. Oh, sir, will you not spare me?

PHILLIP. Spare you, child? You have the power to spare yourself. If you don't want the gentl'man, you have but to say no, and that eends the matter.

JACOB. Not too fast, Phillip. A refusal might lead me to bring matters to a crisis. Please give the matter in question a careful consideration before rendering your decision.

MRS. R. Would you compel us to give you our child in marriage regardless of whether she loved you or not?

JACOB. I trust that my wealth, my social position —

PHILLIP. True love, sir, for the matter of that, have nothing to do with wealth or position. It are the man it wants, wheether he have a dollar or not. Now, Jacob, you say as how you are a man of few words. I be the same. My Mabel shall decide your fate with her own purty lips. If it be "yes" you can have her; but if it be "no," you may as well go home, and may peace go with you. Mabel, do you want this here gentl'man, with his wealth, and position, and other titles, for a husband?

MABEL. Oh, father! you know I can never love him. He surely would not marry me without my love.

PHILLIP. That have nothing to do with the case. A man wot's in love, and desp'rate, would do a'most anything. Come! you must decide your fate, my child, the gentl'man is waiting.

MABEL. O father! I cannot marry him, indeed, I cannot.

PHILLIP. Theer, Jacob, you have your answer — all in a nut-shell. I hope you'll neer be hard on us on that account. He are not much of a man who would marry a girl against her will.

JACOB. Phillip, you are burning your own fingers. Remember, I am not to be thwarted in my designs. I will give you until to-morrow afternoon to think this matter over. At that time, this girl must come to my house with a favorable answer, or the amount of your indebtedness, or the law shall take its course. I wish you a good afternoon. (*Exit* R. U. E.)

PHILLIP. It ain't for me to murmur agin the Lord — it ain't my way; but when he put that theer man together, He made a great mistake. He are nothing but a shark, and we the fish he is after. I had a-hoped it might have been different.

MRS. R. (*weeping*). Oh, Phillip! I knew how it would end. Heaven protect us! what shall we do?

PHILLIP. Well, Betty, just now I am summat timourous about answering. These here eyes of mine — blind as a cave fish — holds me like a boat wot is anchored, and makes me useless. You and Mabel are both strong, and both capable; and with both strength and capability, you can both look into the hereafter with summat of hope. The wust Jacob kin do by me is the sending of me to jail; and that theer thing may be a blessing, for it gives me a bed, and three meals a day, which the like you may not have the happ'ness to get.

MABEL. Oh, he surely cannot be so hard hearted!

PHILLIP. You do not know that theer Jacob, child, so well as your father. I have known him nigh about twenty years, going on, and so much as a particle of goodness I have never found. He will do as he has said.

MABEL. Then I will accept his hand. It shall not be said of me that I was the means of turning you into the streets in your blind and helpless condition.

PHILLIP. Tut! tut! child. You talk in parables; and parables is a language I fail to understand. Come, Betty, lead me into the house. I'm a-going to give this matter a keerful study; and I'm a-going to do it with the Bible upon my knees. I can't read it with these here eyes of mine, but I can think a heap better somehow, when we get kinder associated together. (*They help him from the chair, and he is led into the house by* MRS. RAYMOND.)

MABEL (*watching them off*). O my poor father! I can never live to see him turned into the streets, blind and helpless as he is. If my poor hand can save him, it shall be given. O Edward! Edward! must I give you up? Father of mercy! have compassion upon me, and teach me what to do. (*Throws herself into chair weeping.*)

EDWARD (*enters from* R. U. E., *carrying small bundle*). All this world is but a bubble, and that bubble is full of trouble, with a hubble, and a stubble, and a — (*Perceives Mabel.*) Hello! Mabel, in tears? I didn't think you would weep so soon after learning of my departure.

MABEL (*looking up*). Your departure? Are you going away, Edward?

EDW. Yep! I'm gone; or, that is — I'm most gone. Let me explain. (*Drops bundle, and seats himself opposite* MABEL.) My worthy Uncle called me into his study this morning, and said, "Edward, you are a useless appendage." Admitted. "Edward, you are no longer wanted." Admitted again. "Edward, here is a dollar. Take it, and shift for yourself." Here is the money, Mabel. Take it, I'm afraid of robbery. (*Throws dollar into her lap.*)

MABEL. O Edward! how can you joke on such a solemn occasion.

EDW. Solemn? You just bet it's solemn. But why are you in tears? I dislike tears; and then again, they don't become you.

MABEL (*aside*). Oh, how can I ever tell him! Yet I must! (*Aloud.*) O Edward!. what will you think of me when I tell you we must part forever?

EDW. (*jumping up*). Think of you? By George! I would think you was a mighty queer girl. That's just the way, though. Let a man get cut out of an inheritance, and he gets cut out of everything that wears petticoats.

MABEL. How can you talk so, Edward? You know I would do anything for your sake?

EDW. Yes, until I got the grand bounce, and then leave me.

MABEL. No, no, Edward. Listen to me: Mr. Johnson has been here.

EDW. I know it. I met the old skinflint down the road. Said "good-by" to him as pleasantly as I knew how, and all the old sardine did was just to grin. I see through it, though; money — fine clothes — upper crust — (*Picking up bundle.*) Good-by, Mabel, I'm off.

MABEL (*pulling him back*). Edward, will you listen to me? Mr. Johnson says unless I marry him, or father settles his mortgage, he will turn us into the street; and he even threatens father with something worse.

EDW. (*dropping bundle*). He does — eh? That puts a different face on the matter. How much is the bill? I mean, how much is your father owing him?

MABEL. I hardly know; but it must be in the vicinity of five thousand dollars.

EDW. Whew! then my dollar won't settle it. Snakes! I wish I could plant it and make it grow. Well! (*Pauses.*) Say, Mabel, are you going to marry him?

MABEL. O Edward! what can I do?

EDW. Conundrum! I give it up. You shan't marry that old haddock, though, if the sky falls. (*Noise off* L. U. E.) Hello! what's all that? (ELIAS *enters* L.U.E. *with wheelbarrow loaded with bundles, etc. He is followed by boys, who throw sticks at him, and shout, "Murderer! Coward! Fool!"*)

They upset his wheelbarrow near front of stage. EDWARD *interferes.*) Clear out! Have you no more manners than to pick upon a poor fellow who is minding his own business? Away with you, or I'll show you what a full-blooded Yankee is made of. (*They run off* L. U. E., *shouting " Coward! Murderer !" etc.*)

(ELIAS, *assisted by* MABEL, *rights wheelbarrow and bundles.* ELIAS *seats himself on handle of wheelbarrow, as* EDWARD *comes down front.* MABEL *remains* R.)

ELIAS (*much affected*). Poor Elias ha' not got many friends, Edward.

EDW. Well, he's got one, and don't you forget it. And if I'm not mistaken, he has another in Mabel here.

ELIAS. Yes; Mabel be a friend t' Elias, Mabel be. Once I had the fever. It wus in a room down there in the old mill; an' no one would come a-near of me; an' I wus left t' die. But one day, Mabel comes, an' watches over me, an' cares for me till the fever had turned, an' I was well again. I ha' not forgotten it, Edward.

MABEL. And richly have I been rewarded by your close attendance to the mill since my father's blindness. Your faithfulness and careful management have been the sole means of keeping the family together.

EDW. You just bet it has. Still, Elias, you stand abuse like a western mule. Are you a coward? No; you proved your courage when you saved Higgins' child from drowning. To repay you he orders you out of the house. How is that for an exemplification of humanity?

ELIAS. Higgins be not the only man who ha' turned me from his house. But it be all right; I ha' got used t' trouble, Edward.

EDW. Well, so have I. You see, without going into details, that skinflint of a Johnson has been here and snarled things up generally.

ELIAS (*rising agitated*). What be that ye ha' said? Johnson been here? Ha' that man Johnson been here?

EDW. Of course he has. Don't you see the atmosphere is clouded? It hasn't cleared up since he left.

MABEL. It is true, Elias; and he had the impudence to ask me to become his wife.

EDW. And all the time, recollect, she was pledged to me.

ELIAS (*greatly agitated*). You become his wife! Say it slow — say it slow, Mabel. I fear I ha' made a mistake. You become the wife of Jacob Johnson?

MABEL. He has said it, Elias. He is determined that I shall marry him.

ELIAS (*slow, and with much feeling*). He — Jacob Johnson — marry you? You who ha' been a friend t' me? Who ha' cared for me when I wus sick? Who ha' been like a sister t' me? You become the wife of that man? Ye shall not do it, Mabel, ye shall not do it!

MABEL. But to refuse is to turn my poor parents into the street.

ELIAS. Ye be not turned into the streets — not while Elias lives. Run in now — I ha' a word t' say t' Edward. (*Leads her toward door.*) Run in, and remember I be a-working for ye. (MABEL *exit into house.* ELIAS *comes down.*) Edward, I ha' a question t' ask, an' then ye can follow Mabel. If ye love her, an' I ha' reason t' think that ye do, meet me at dark to-night at my room down there in the old mill. (*Grasping his arm.*) I ha' a surprise for ye, Edward.

EDW. Well, I've had two already, and it will take a galvanic battery to give me another. However, I'll be there, and don't you forget it.

ELIAS. Ye shall not regret it, Edward, ye shall not regret it. Run in now, for Mabel be in waiting. (*Leads him toward door.*) Run in an' tell Phillip I be mad; that a volcano has sprung up in my bosom; that poor, simple Elias will save him, or the God he ha' worshipped ha' turned against him. (EDWARD *exit into house.* ELIAS *comes down front.*) Oh! that I had the tongue t' speak, I would use it now. I would expose that accursed fiend t' the eyes of the world, or perish in the attempt. (SETH RANDOLPH *enters* R. U. E. *unperceived.*) Alas! I cannot. My word is given, an' when I give my word, it is a covenant not t' be broken. I will keep my oath! (*Turns to take wheelbarrow, and perceives* SETH, *whom he recognizes. Chord. They stare at each other for a moment in silence.*)

SETH. Well! what are you staring at? Are you aware that he who leers at another shows a breeding of ill manners? Besides, it places a gentleman like myself in a very embarrassing position.

ELIAS. Ye be no gentleman, sir.

SETH. No gentleman? Insult added to contumely. My friend, ignorance has calloused your judgment. If I am no gentleman, for Heaven's sake! what am I?

ELIAS (*pointing at him with finger*). Ye be a murderer, Seth Randolph.

SETH (*starting back*). Damnation! exposed! For God's sake! who are you?

ELIAS. Elias Amsden, the boy ye bound by an oath. (*Picture.*)

CURTAIN.

ACT II.

SCENE I. — *Interior of mill. Divided stage, showing two rooms in same flat. Room to the* R., *contains old cot, stool, stand, and lighted candle. Above cot is small window. Trap door,* C. *Entrance* R. C. *Room to* L. *contains cot, old stool, stand, etc. Entrance* L. C. *Middle partition shows opening for box stove. This opening is closed with boards arranged to be moved. If convenient, pulleys and belts should project into rooms. Time, evening. At rise of curtain* ELIAS *is discovered in room to* R. *He sits opposite stand, with his head resting upon it. Music at opening.*

(SETH RANDOLPH *enters room to* L.)

SETH (*feeling in his pockets*). Where did I put that candle? Oh, here it is! (*Takes candle from his pocket.*) Now for a light. (*Lights candle and tries to balance it on table.*) That won't work! Well, must have a candlestick somehow. (*Perceives tumbler.*) Here! I'll substitute this. (*Puts candle in tumbler and jams paper around it.*) There! there's a candlestick worthy of a patent. (*Examines room.*) This is no drawing-room; but it is safer than abiding with Jacob, if I do own half of the establishment. (*Seating himself at stand.*) Ugh! that boy gave me the shakes. He will not expose me, though, and Jacob dare not, so I have nothing to fear. (*Yawns.*) Well, I'll have a smoke, and then retire. (*Takes out pipe, lights it, and leans back smoking. Loud rap at door in opposite room.*) Hello! I guess I'm going to have neighbors. (*Knock repeated.*)

ELIAS (*rising, and going toward door*). I be a-coming, Edward, I be a-coming. (*Opens door.* EDWARD *enters.*) I thought as how ye would not disappoint me. (*They come down.*)

EDWARD. Disappoint you? No; not when there 's anything at stake. (*Sits down on cot and looks around.*) Whew! this is a gloomy hole. Arn't you afraid of ghosts?

ELIAS (*sitting on stool*). I be no believer in ghosts, Edward, unless they be clothed in flesh an' bone. I be haunted enough by them already. Ha' ye found out how much Raymond be owing?

EDW.   It knocks the spots off from five thousand dollars.
Mabel and I figured it up after you left.   I haven't seen
figures look so gloomy since the day I figured fractions in
school when I wanted to go fishing.   Every one loomed up
just like a thunder-cloud. .

SETH.   Their talk has a flavoring of money in it; and if
anything can send a thrill like electricity through me, it is
money.   I'll draw up a little nearer.   (*Moves up to opening
in partition and listens.*)

ELIAS.   Edward, I be going t' tell ye a secret, an' I ha'
the confidence in ye that ye will keep it.   That I know the
murderers o' the man that wus found, ye be well aware; an'
ye know I ha' been put t' a'most every test t' compel me t'
expose 'em.   I ha' been threatened, an' kicked, an' abused,
until I be not the same as formerly, either in body or mind.
I be a man, though, for all o' that; an' I ha' a heart like as
other men; an' there be feelin' in that heart; an' it be
tender.   It be that tender, Edward, that often of a night,
when I be here alone, an' everything be still — all but the
water of the river out there — that I ha' wept, an' I ha' done
it often.   But I be constrained by an oath.   I ha' often
wished I had died afore I had taken it; but that be too late.
I ha' taken the oath, an' I be bound t' keep it.

SETH (*aside, listening*).   Thank the Lord for that!

ELIAS (*continuing*).   The secret I have for ye, be not
one relating t' the oath, but one that will interest ye far
more.   (*Rising.*)   Wait but a moment, Edward, an' I will
come back.   (*Goes to trap, which he opens, and descends.*)

EDW.   Poor fellow! I believe his brain is turned without
a doubt.   What the deuce can he have in that wheel pit
that's going to be of any interest to me? I'm all of a
muddle.

SETH.   That fellow convinces me that I am more of a
brute than I gave myself credit for.   That, however, is just
the way.   The man who builds up too good an opinion of
himself, will frequently get that opinion shattered when least
expected.   Out of evil, evil springs, no matter how you white-
wash it over.   (*Listens.*)

(ELIAS *emerges from trap with small box.   He returns
front.*)

ELIAS. The night afore my father died, he called me t'
his bedside, an' said, "Elias, ye ha' been a good lad, but ye
ha' a secret about ye that's a-going t' be the ruin o' your life.
So long as ye keep it, ye will ha' no friends, an' ye will live
in torment wid yourself;" an' it has been a fact. (*Opens box
and takes out wallet*.) Then he takes this wallet from
underneath his pillow, an' he says, "Elias, ye will need
money sometime, an' money will be a friend t' ye when ye
ha' no other. I ha' saved a little in my day, an' I be now
going t' make it a present t' you. When I be gone," that's
what he said; "when I be gone, an' be placed beside your
mother, get the money out o' the place, an' put it with this.
Then ye hide it away until your mind be righted, or ye ha' a
friend in whom ye can trust it." This wallet, Edward, contains over five thousand dollars, an' the time ha' now come t'
use it. To-morrow ye can settle Phillip's notes, an' by the
doing of it release Mabel from all further persecution of that
man.

EDW. (*grasping his hand*). Elias, I — I — Well — I —
Dash it all! you've choked me all up. You're gold, that's
what you are, real gold. B-blast it! you're better than gold.
You're a trump! How can I ever thank —

ELIAS (*putting wallet back into box*). I want no thanks,
Edward. It be a pleasure for me t' assist ye. Ye ha' always
been a friend t' me, an' I ha' not forgotten it. Wait, now,
an' I will return this box. Then I will bid ye a good-night.
(*Takes box and descends into trap*.)

EDW. Why, that poor fellow is all heart. Over five
thousand dollars in his possession, and no one knew it!
That beats me. To know that we can beat that old haddock
— why, I could hug that poor fellow closer than a bear.
(*Jumps up and walks floor*.)

(SETH *has slowly risen from his seat, comes down front,
pauses, turns back, then returns front again as* EDWARD
ceases speaking.)

SETH. If the devil ever took pains to tempt one man
more than another, I am that man. Here is an opportunity
to strike, and yet, my heart rebels against it. (*Seats himself on stool meditating.* ELIAS *emerges from trap*.)

ELIAS. It has been said, Edward, that I ha' been hired

t' keep that secret. That I ha' not been hired, I solemnly
attest; an' I ha' the God that watches me t' witness it.
Now ye can go t' Mabel. Say nothing t' her about this
matter, an' when the time arrives, ye can give her a happy
surprise. Good night, Edward, an' may ye rest the better
for what I ha' told ye.

EDW. (*grasping his hand*). Elias, I'm stuck for
words to express my thanks. All I can say is, if I could
knock those murderers into a cocked hat, and relieve your
mind of this burden, I'd do it, so help me Jeremiah! (*Exit
C. D.*)

ELIAS. I would that ye had the power, Edward, I would
that ye had the power. (*Closes door, returns, and sits upon
edge of cot. Moonlight through window shines upon him during
the following.*) I remember when I wus a wee bit of a lad,
that one summer night, as I wus a-weeping over the loss of
some childish toy, my mother took me upon her knee, an'
after kissing the tears away with her own loving lips, she
said, "You be grieved to-night, my child, an' all over a
trivial matter. If you grow t' manhood," an' I can remember how she looked when she said it — looked with her
great brown eyes, — "if you grow t' manhood," she said,
"you will encounter trouble, as must all who live the
longest. An' when it comes, you will look back t' this
moment — this little period of grief," as she called it, "an'
find it t' be the happiest hour of your life." Oh, how faith-
fully ha' the words come true that she uttered; for to-night,
if that childhood's hour could come back t' me, it would be
all the earthly heaven I would ask. (*Rises and arranges
furniture, cot, etc.*) There be not much comfort in sleep,
an' yet it be necessary t' live. I be threatened with death
by Jacob, an' now his confederate he comes, an' there be a
new danger. He be the lesser villain o' the two, an' yet he
be a villain, so I ha' nothing t' hope. O Jacob! Jacob! ye
ha' murdered one, an' ye be a-killing another by inches.
(*Extinguishes candle, and throws himself upon couch.
Dark stage.*)

SETH (*who has risen from stool and advanced front*).
Seth, you old rascal, you are getting womanish. You want
that money, and you don't want it. You know if you take
it you are a damned villain; and you know if you let it

alone you will always curse yourself. Query! shall I take it, or shall I not. (*Pause.*) Well, I'm going to let the coin decide. (*Takes a copper from his pocket.*) If it turns up heads, the die is cast; but if it turns up tails, I'm an honest man. Now, Seth, cheat the Devil once in your life, and reform. (*Snaps copper. Picks it up and looks at it.*) Just as I expected — I'm booked for another crime. Well, once I extricated myself from a like difficulty, and methinks I can again. (*Takes wallet from his pocket, opens it, and takes out large roll of bills.*) Here are ten thousand dollars in this one roll — all counterfeit. I know it because I helped engrave 'em myself. I will steal that money, because I need it; but I will replace it dollar for dollar with this. Before the deception is discovered, I will be out of the country. Eureka! what a thought! (*Returns wallet to his pocket. Takes out dark lantern and lights it.*) Now, Seth, catch the hunter asleep and steal his gun. (*Goes to opening in partition and listens. Music.*) All seems to be quiet. Now to gain access to the room. (*Slowly removes boards and looks into room.*) The coast is clear. (*Cautiously enters room. Stops and listens, then slowly lifts trap-door and descends. As trap-door closes,* ELIAS *starts, sits upright and looks around. Music.*)

ELIAS. It be but a dream! it be but a dream! (*Sighs, then sinks back upon couch.*)

SETH (*slowly raises trap, partly emerges and looks around*). He still sleeps. Now for my own room. (*Closes trap, cautiously enters his own room and replaces boards.*) There! everything is as I found it. (*Advances front.*) Well, Seth, you have made the exchange; but you have lowered yourself in your own estimation. (*Holding up money and looking at it.*) O money! money! you are the bane of my life; but I worship you as a God. (SETH *stands with money held aloft.* ELIAS *sits upright as if listening. Scene closes in.*)

SCENE II. — *Highway.*

(SAMBO *enters from* L. *carrying box and large bundle. He is followed by* LUCY *with bundles.*)

SAMBO (*looking back*). Come — come along, dar. Can't

wait all day, Missey Lucy. Dis yer child gwine to go home sometime fo' break of sunset.

LUCY. For the land sakes don't hurry so. Give me that box tu sit down on, can't ye? (SAMBO *places box* C.) I'm clean gone tuckered tu death. (*Sits down on box.*) There! now you jest wait till I catch my breath, an' then I'll trudge along.

SAMBO. How you gwine to cotch it, Missey Lucy, wid a hook? Lor a mighty Mas'r Johnson tole me to help you over wid the tings, and stiver right back. 'Specks I cotch um something besides breff if I don't recommmember his orders.

LUCY. Well, Jacob won't break his puckering string if he waits. Land a massey! this world wern't recreated in a minute. Let him fret. I'm a-goin' tu rest if the hull world sees me.

SAMBO. 'Spects you are, Missey Lucy, 'spects you are. Lor a mighty! dar's nuffin under de sun more stubborn den a woman — 'cept a mule. Dat's a fact.

LUCY. An' there's nuthin under the sun blacker than a nigger. If Drucill can afford tu give me these things, I guess you can afford tu help carry 'em; an' there ain't no use makin' sech a fuss about it either. I didn't intend to stay all night; but Drucill resisted upon it so, that I consented. Land a massy! I didn't see anything at Jacob's that you told about! There wasn't so much as a stranger about the house. You niggers will lie the wust of any people I ever did see.

SAMBO. You doan know nuffin 'bout it. What you say am a 'spursion on de black man's character. Didn't that shootin' popperer shovel-de-freeze de compartment? Ain't dem holes dar in de partition made by de bullets? Did you see 'em, Missey Lucy?

LUCY See 'em — yes; an' asked Drucilla all about 'em. She said they wus made by moths — nuthin under the sun but moths. An' she said if they didn't git some kind of consarvitive, they'd bore the hull house down about their heads. I told her if they got under the keerpet tu jest dust some pellmation in an' that would fix 'em. Pellmation an' helenbore are the best consarvatives for moths I ever did see. You jest write that down, Samuel, an' remember it.

SAMBO (*excited*). A-a-a-and Missey Drucilla said dat dem yer holes in de partition wus made by mofs?

LUCY. Why, of course she did. Is there anything so awfully wonderful about that?

SAMBO. Dar ain't nuffin wonderful 'bout it — nuffin wonderful 't all. I wus jess a-tinkin.' I wus a-tinkin' if dem bullet-holes in de partition wus made by mofs, what dey would be called if dey wus made by cannon-balls.

LUCY. Why, cannon-ball holes, of course. Sech stupidity I never did see. Here! (*Noticing SAMBO who has been resting first on one foot and then the other.*) If you are gettin' tired, you kin have one eend of this box. I don't like tu see ye teeterin' fust on one foot an' then on t'other.

SAMBO. (*edging off*). N-no-no! thank'ee, Missey Lucy. I'se no squatter. I, I kin stan' — I kin.

LUCY. Well, then for Massey's sake du stand still. I'm not particular about sittin' broadside tu a nigger anyway. It was only out of a generous compulse that I asked ye. I don't keer nuthin about it, I hope you don't think, not a thing.

SAMBO (*edging back*). Lor-a-mighty! I isn't afeard to sit alongside of yer! Dat isn't the reason I refused, Missey Lucy. Dat isn't the reason 't all. It am de fact dat de box am of such small kervacity dat I might crowd yer. I doan want to crowd yer, Missey Lucy.

LUCY (*hitching along*). Well, I kin hitch along, can't I? I won't bite, if you are a nigger. (*Hitches to L. with back to C.*

SAMBO. Den dis yer chile will occupy de seat. (*Sits down carefully on box, and faces R. while LUCY faces L. Box must contain glass, and so arranged as to break down.*) Dar! dar! I'se here. Mus, look out fo' de bearings, though, or dar 'llbe a bustification sure. (*Braces himself as if expecting to fall.*)

LUCY. Land a massey! du you think this box won't hold? Why, it is strong as — (*Jounces up and down on box which suddenly collapses, and all go down together. Sound of broken glass.*) Gracious Peter! there goes the glass-ware! For mercy's sake help me out of this! (*SAMBO jumps up and assists LUCY.*) I never did see sech an awkward, stupid, clumsy, dodunk of a stick as a nigger is.

SAMBO. Dar ain't nuffin stupid 'bout a nigger. Dey's got jess as much brain as a white man. I tole you dat de box wouldn't hold? I tole you all about it.

LUCY (*picking up things*). Well, if you hadn't sot down like a spile-driver it would a held. A box can't hold everything no more nor a museum. Come! pick up your traps an' we'll trudge along.

SAMBO (*picking up remnants of box and bundles*). Don't care nuffin' bout de traps — nuffin 't all. Dis yer chile gets blamed fo' most ebberyting, 'Spects if a streak of lightning should hit yer, dat dis yer chile would have to take de consequences.

LUCY (*going* R.) Well, crawl out through a gimlet hole if you want tu. If you had kept off from the box, it wouldn't a broke. Now the tea-set Drucilla gave me is smashed, an' I haven't another tu replace it. (*Exit* R.)

SAMBO (*following her*). Lor' a-mighty! who crushed de tea-set? Who broke down de box? Who wus de cause of de carastophe dat discombobolated de equilibrium of de consarn? Who— (*Goes off* R.)

(*Scene changes.*)

SCENE III. — *Room in* JOHNSON'S *house same as in Act I.,
Scene I.*

JACOB (*seated at table* L. *Looks at watch*). Ten minutes of two, and that girl has not arrived. If she disappoints me now, it will be worse with her than she is aware of. Curse the luck! everything of late works in opposition to my wishes. The return of that scoundrel portends no good of itself. He knows too much about me. I dare not oppose him, for he has me completely in his power. He has taken a room in Raymond's mill. Elias occupies the one next to it. By one bold stroke I could spring a trap upon them that would dispose of both of them at once. It shall be done. I will set the trap, and spring it, or my name is not Jacob Johnson.

(DRUCILLA *enters* R. 3 E.)

DRUCILLA (*coming down*). Mr. Johnson, I wish an explanation as to the conduct of that vagabond you are so freely entertaining. Bless me! he seems to run the establishment; eating and drinking, damaging the furniture, abusing the servants, in fact, doing just as he pleases, while you coolly remain seated, and let him do it. Now why is this the case, I would like to ask?

JACOB. Well, Drucilla, the fact is, I — Well-er-you see, we were friends together when I was in the East. I tolerate him on that account. Quite likely I put up with more from him than I would from others for those simple reasons.

DRU. Quite likely; but I have my doubts about the matter. I know this much, he is wearing out his welcome; at least, he is with me; and if you haven't the courage to turn him out, I shall take the case into my own hands. I won't stand it, I tell you.

JACOB. Well, well, Drucilla, have a little patience. It is possible he may disappear as suddenly as he came. It is better to have the good-will of such a fellow, than the ill-will, if it does discommode us at times. Have patience, Drucilla.

DRU. I'm all out of patience, I tell you. Now I want to know another thing. How did you succeed with that silly courtship of yours? Not very satisfactory I should judge, if your looks are any indications.

JACOB. More satisfactory, perhaps, than you may think. She is to render me her decision this afternoon. By the way, Drucilla, would it meet with your displeasure to retire when she arrives? Such matters, you know, can be better adjusted without the presence of a third party.

DRU. O yes, I can go. I might know I shouldn't be wanted. I have no desire to witness such silly nonsense — it is far beneath me. As I can hear a step in the hall, perhaps I had better retire at once. You may be glad enough for my advice before you get through with the matter. (*Exit* R. 3 E.)

SAMBO (*enters* C.). Here am a card, Mas'r Johnson. (*Gives card.*)

JACOB (*glancing at card*). The young lady in question. (*To* SAMBO.) You can admit her. (SAMBO *exit* C.) Now I soon shall know if there is a second refusal in store for me.

(SAMBO *ushers in* MABEL, *after which, he remains standing in archway* C. MABEL *comes down front.*)

MABEL. You desired me to bring my answer this afternoon. I now am here to fulfil that promise.

JACOB. Yes, yes, I understand. (*Advancing, and placing chair.*) Please be seated. (*Both sit.*) After carefully considering the matter, you have concluded to render me a favorable decision. Well, your decision is wise. You can dress well, live at ease, and I will liquidate your father's burdensome debts.

MABEL. I fear, sir, you do not quite understand me. I have called to plead with you — plead with you as only a woman can for her parent's welfare. Oh, sir, you cannot be so cruel as to turn them into the street because a simple girl is unable to love you! Surely, sir, you cannot.

JACOB. Really, Miss Raymond, I was not expecting this. I have been very lenient toward your father, very. As for yourself, you know I cherish for you a very ardent affection.

MABEL. Then let that affection restrain you from acting unjustly. Let it lead you to be merciful, and you will have the heartfelt thanks of an unfortunate family. Abandon the promise you would forcibly extract from me, and Heaven, I know, will reward you.

JACOB. Quite impossible. I am only performing my duty. A duty, which, but for my love for you, would, ere this, have led me to more stringent measures. I considered that my offer of marriage would be regarded as an honor. As you see fit to regard it otherwise, you must not blame me for taking advantage of the privilege allowed me by law.

MABEL. And that privilege means to turn us forth into a pitiless world, homeless and friendless. Oh, sir, do not add another sorrow to a home that is already saddened. Allow us a little time — a year is all we ask. Allow us that, and if God will answer our prayers we will endeavor to meet your demands.

JACOB. Miss Raymond, this is idle talk. Accept my hand, and all goes well with you. Refuse, and the law shall take its course. I have spoken.

MABEL. And you would marry me regardless of my love? Are you aware that I could never make you happy?

JACOB. The risk is mine if I see fit to take it. You will learn to love me as an adopted child learns to love its new parents. But why this silly argument? The sooner you decide this question, the sooner we shall understand each other,

MABEL. Will nothing change your mind?

JACOB. No power under Heaven.

MABEL (*aside*). O my poor father, forgive me for what I am about to do. (*Rising from chair; aloud.*) Jacob Johnson, listen to me. If God ever .gave a man a heart without one thrill of compassion in it, He has given it to you: for you are a tyrant in all its forms so far as you dare exercise it. If, knowing that I despise you; knowing that I hate you as only a woman can hate, you then will accept my hand —

(SETH *enters* C. *unperceived by* SAMBO, *takes him by the ear and starts front.*)

SAMBO (*crying out*). Hi dar! —git out! Dis yer chile ain't done nuffin! Let go dat ear, Mas'r Somebody. Let go, I tole yer.

SETH (*whirling him over to* C. R.). Never obstruct the highway, Erebus, as you value your life. The laws of the country are against it.

SAMBO (*holding on to his ear*). Hain't distructed no high-way. Hain't done nuffin to cause any such salt and buttery attack. Dis yer chile wus minding his own business.

JACOB (*who has risen from chair, and is almost unable to control his anger*). Sir! sir! do you perceive that this interview is strictly private?

SETH. I do, Jacob, and that my presence has disturbed you. However, don't mind me. Consider me one of the family; an obsolete member, so to speak. Continue your courtship, Jacob, I'll sit down over here and read the news. (*Sits down* R. H. C. *and takes paper from his pocket.*)

JACOB. It is my desire that you leave the room. When this interview has terminated you can return.

SETH. Yes, that is quite rational. The son goes out at night, and returns in the morning. The hard earned dollar goes out, but never returns. A good sentinel stands by his post. I'll guard you, Jacob, and if you are overpowered, I'll take your place. Go on, Jacob, go on. (*Reads.*)

JACOB (*controlling his anger*). Rather than create a dis-turbance, I will tolerate your presence. Remember, though, you are not wanted. (*To* MABEL.) Miss Raymond, am I to understand from your uncomplimentary remarks that my offer was accepted?

MABEL. Will no power under Heaven cause you to release me?

JACOB. No; I tell you. It shall be your hand, or the money, if it breaks a thousand hearts.

MABEL. Then, sir, release my parents, and though my life is ruined, you can have my hand —

EDWARD (*rushing in, followed by* ELIAS). No he can't! (*Chord. All start.* EDWARD *crosses to* MABEL, *and clasps her in his arms.* ELIAS *remains* C.)

JACOB. Damnation!

EDW. Mabel, I've come to save you. I'm going to knock the bottom out of those notes, or break the bank. (*To* JACOB.) Come, Jacob, trot them out, and I'll settle them in the wink of a bird's eye.

JACOB. There is treachery at the bottom of this. What brings you here, and in the company of that man? (*Points to* ELIAS.)

EDW. An honest impulse brings me here. I've come to settle Raymond's notes.

ELIAS. An' I be come t' witness the settlement.

JACOB. You witness the settlement of Raymond's notes? So, so, I perceive — I perceive! (*Sarcastically.*) Even fools know how to conspire.

ELIAS. I be no fool, Jacob Johnson.

MABEL. O Edward! where did you get the money?

EDW. It matters not, Mabel, so long as I came by it honestly. I will explain at another time. (*To* JACOB.) Come! the quicker you trot out those notes the better. This atmosphere is contagious.

JACOB. Pooh! what have you to do with Raymond's notes? Bah! you couldn't raise a dollar to save your life.

EDW. Couldn't — eh? You just figure up your claim, and I'll cover it with as handsome bank-bills as your snaky eyes ever gazed at. Oh, I've got the money, and don't you forget it!

SETH (*down* R. I. E.). Never refuse money, Jacob, when it is offered you. It is imprudent, as I have learned from past experience.

JACOB. What is it to you? (*Aside.*) Curse the luck! they are all linked together.

DRUCILLA (*enters* R. 3. E. *Looks around astonished*).

Well, I declare! Is this a celebration? A pretty private interview, indeed! Jacob, why have you deceived me in this matter? Why are these people here?

JACOB. They have intruded themselves upon me without my consent. They are scheming to ruin me; but they shall find me equal to the emergency. I will outwit the whole of them. (*Goes down* L. *to secretary, which he opens, and looks for papers.*)

DRU. (*down* C. L.). Indeed! a conspiracy? I do not wonder at it. The character you have entertained for the past few days is capable of plotting anything.

SETH. Madam, behold in me a monument of innocence. All I can say is, that present procedures relate to money, and — most everything does.

ELIAS. We be here t' settle Raymond's notes, an' save his daughter. She be not agoin t' marry Jacob.

EDW. You're just shouting she ain't.

DRU. Indeed! is she not capable of managing her own affairs? Jacob, will you please render an explanation of all this? I am surprised! astonished! Sambo, fan me. (*Hands* SAMBO *large fan, which he uses.*)

JACOB. (*returning to table with papers*). My explanation is this: These people think to intimidate me; but they have mistaken their man (*To* EDWARD.) Now, sir, you claim to have money. Well, then, here are Raymond's notes. (*Places notes on table.*) The total amount, with interest added, is five thousand five hundred and fifty dollars. Count out that amount upon this table in American currency, and they belong to you. I defy you to do it. (*Straightens back defiantly.*)

EDW. Defy a Le Roy? By the blade that killed Cæsar, the lamb shall outwit the lion. Here! give me room according to my strength. (*Advancing to table.*) I remember when I was turned from the house with but a single dollar. I planted that dollar, it took root, sprung up, budded and blossomed. Here, Mr. Johnson, is the fruit. (*Takes out large package of bills and flourishes them over the table.*)

JACOB (*aside*), Curses light on him! where did he get that money!

EDW. Now, sir, prepare to count. (*Spreads out money on table. All, with the exception of* SETH, *form circle around him.*)

SETH (*aside* R. I E.). The decisive moment has arrived. If the deception is not discovered, I have made a strike. If detected, I have been the cause of more ruin than a. dynamite bomb. (*Watches count.*)

(EDWARD *places seven packages on table, five of which are divided into ten lesser ones. He breaks open two of them, and spreads the contents out.*)

EDW. There! you see what it is to have money. Five of these packages are divided into ten each. Each package contains one hundred dollars. That makes five thousand. The balance is in these other two. You see, sir, we have figured these notes as well as yourself. Count it, and if correct, fulfil your part of the contract. (*For a moment* JABOB *stands as if puzzled how to act. Then he reaches out and takes package from table.*)

MABEL. O Edward! Edward! how can I ever thank you? Who has thought so much of my poor father as to ever befriend him like this? Oh, tell me, that I may kneel before him and bless him.

EDW. Your deliverer stands there. (*Points to* ELIAS. *Chord.*)

(*All show great surprise and look at* ELIAS. SETH *alone appears unconcerned.*)

MABEL. What! Elias? (*Crossing to* ELIAS *and grasping him by the hand.*) O Elias! are you such a friend to me as this? I thought you to be as poor as ourselves. Oh, how can we ever thank you?

ELIAS. Ye ha' no one t' thank, Mabel. I be but doing my duty by ye. I ha' nothing t' say about the money— Edward can explain that as he ha' a mind. (*Looking sharply at* SETH *and* JACOB.) It be not money obtained by crime, though, or by any lawless act that ye could blush at.

(*During the above,* JACOB *has been slowly counting the money. Suddenly he stops, takes a bill, looks at it carefully, turns it over, scrutinizes it closely, and does the same with others.* SETH *watches him and grows greatly excited. At last,* JACOB *goes to secretary, takes out a book and brings it to table. Business of looking in book and comparing bills. At last, apparently satisfied, he lays down the book, gathers up the* RAYMOND *notes and puts them in his pocket. This latter movement is noticed by* EDWARD.)

EDW. How, now! what means that act? Is not the count correct?

JACOB (*smiling*). Certainly; even to a dollar. I congratulate you on your success.

EDW. Of course you do. A man with half a heart would do that; but why are you so free about pocketing those notes?

JACOB. For reasons which you too readily understand. (*Pointing to money.*) Every dollar of that money is as worthless as the paper it is printed on.

ELIAS. } What!
EDWARD. }

JACOB. I say, every dollar of that money is a base counterfeit.

ELIAS (*wildly*). You lie! you lie! Jacob Johnson. It be good, every dollar of it, an' I will take me oath t' it.

DRU. (*excitedly*). Fan me — fan me, Sambo.

SETH (*starts forward as if to speak, and then falls back; aside*). No; I dare not. O God! what a brute I am! Curses light on me for stealing that money.

JACOB. Take your oath to it, will you? Here! look at this? (*Holds up book and compares bills.*) Look in the book and then at the bills. Compare the signature. Look at the print. The texture of the paper. Ha! ha! ha! they are as beautiful a lot of counterfeits as was ever in print.

MABEL (*clinging to* EDWARD). Oh, Edward! Edward!

DRU. Fan me, Sambo.

ELIAS (*trembling with rage*). Jabob! Jacob! ye be a crazing of me. Ye be makin' me desperate. Ye be tearin' from my lips —

JACOB (*affrighted, and starting forward*). Elias Amsden, beware!

ELIAS (*starting back*). Oh, I be doomed — doomed!

CURTAIN.

(*Disposition of characters.*)

ELIAS.

MABEL. DRUCILLA.

EDWARD. SAMBO.

SETH. (*Table.*) JACOB.

R. L.

ACT III.

SCENE I. — *Room in* JOHNSON'S *house same as in Act I.,
and Act II. As curtain rises,* SAMBO *is discovered standing in center of room.*

SAMBO. Lor a-mighty! but I'se a gwine to vacate dese
yer premises sure. Ebbery ting 'pears to be helter-skelter
lately. Mas'r Johnson acts as if the debbil wus in him, and
Missy Drucilla — she jess galvinates round de 'stablishment
as if she wus stung wid a hornet, and Mas'r Raymond —
mighty sorry 'bout him — turned into de streets to-day —
right into de streets wid his family, and Mas'r Edward, he
done gone and runed away — can't find him nowheres, and
dat yer shootin' popperer ain't de same at all — don't say
nuffin to nobody — why, I can't see through it nohow.
'Spect's it am a judgment on dis yer community. Bress de
Lord! but I'se agwine to trabbel afore it reckons me in wid
de rest of de family. I is, sure's you're born.

DRUCILLA (*enters* c.). What is this muttering about, I
should like to inquire!

SAMBO (*starting*). Hi dar! Why, Missey Drucilla, de
furniture is all displaced. Takes dis chile de whole time
lately to keep dis compartment in 'spectable condition.
(*Arranges furniture.*)

DRU. Indeed! well, you have nothing else to do.
Where is your master?

SAMBO. Doan know — doan know nuffin 'bout it. 'Spect's
he am wid dat shootin' popperer somewheres. 'Pears to
take mighty sight of interest in him lately, Mas'r Johnson
does.

DRU. That vagabond, indeed. He's a good-for-nothing
villain, if I'm any judge of character. Tell Jacob, when he
arrives, that I wish to speak with him. (*Exit* R. 3 E.)

SAMBO. I'll tole him — I'll tole him, Missey Drucilla.
Lor a-mighty! it won't mount to nuffin, though. Dat man
am de contraritest critter — why, he won't do nuffin dat's
wanted of him, nuffin tall. Ya! ya! ya! he says Missey
Drucilla's tongue am like a perennial spring; allus on de run.
'Spect's it am a fact, 'cause it has nebber dried up since my
connection wid the family.

(*Enter* JACOB JOHNSON *followed by* SETH.)

JACOB. Sambo, take this letter to whom it is addressed.
(*Gives letter.*)

SAMBO. Yis, sah! yis, sah! I'se jess ready to fly, sah.
(*Pauses.*)

JACOB. Well, why don't you fly?

SAMBO. Missey Drucilla wants to speak wid you a minute.

JACOB. Well, Drucilla can wait. Now do as I command you.

SAMBO. Yis, sah! I'se gone, sah! (*Exit* C.)

JACOB. Seth, please be seated. (SETH *sits* R. *of table*, JACOB L.) I have a few remarks to make.

SETH. Make them, Jacob.

JACOB. It is evident that we understand each other thoroughly. That knowledge informs us that we are two villains.

SETH. It does, Jacob, with this exception. One has a conscience, and the other hasn't.

JACOB. Pooh! your conscience must be a curious combination. It certainly is, to make you repentant one night, and a counterfeiter the next.

SETH (*partly rising*). What!

JACOB. Seth, the money that was paid on those notes was counterfeit, and you knew it. I now am convinced of it from the fact that I have a letter in my possession, which you dropped, showing your connection with as sharp a band of counterfeiters as there is in the country.

SETH (*agitated*). Jacob, give me that letter.

JACOB. Never! it is of too much importance.

SETH. Give me that letter, I tell you. (*Starts to draw revolver.* JACOB *watches his movements and covers him first.*)

JACOB. Take away your hand — take it away. (SETH *reluctantly lets go of revolver.*) For once in our career I stand at the head. (*Places his revolver on edge of table.*) Now listen. This letter balances the paper in your possession which you compelled me to write and sign. Exchange with me, and we have only verbal proof of each other's guilt.

SETH. No; when I yield up that paper, my power over you has weakened. As for that letter, you dare not use it, so I have nothing to fear. Don't rouse the demon within me, Jacob, because if you do I shall be dangerous.

JACOB. You have nothing to fear from me. My revenge shall fall upon those who paid me that money.

SETH. But the ones who paid you that money are innocent.

JACOB. Nevertheless, unless that girl accepts my hand, they shall suffer.

SETH. Shall?

JACOB. I have said it. They are completely in my power.

SETH. Is your power over them greater than the power of that lad over us?

JACOB. Bah! that lad is demented. A full confession from him would be regarded with no more weight than a feather.

SETH. Be not too sure, Jacob. The weight of an argument is not felt until each sentence has been carefully analyzed. I tell you, the confession of that lad would send us to the gallows. At least, beware how you irritate him, for it is in opposition to my wishes.

JACOB. Seth, you would work against me?

SETH. Well, my heart is touched. Through me that family has been ruined. I stole that money. D'ye hear? I stole every dollar of it and replaced it with counterfeit. We together, Jacob, have been the cause of much mischief. For my part I am sorry. To-morrow, if God spares my life, I will return that money, and they can settle those notes as was their intention.

JACOB. And by so doing you would cheat me out of the girl. Seth, you don't mean it.

SETH (*striking table with his fist*). I do mean it, so help me God! (*Rises, and goes down* R. I E.)

JACOB (*aside*). Curse him! he would ruin me. Before to-morrow arrives, he shall be a dead man. (*Aloud.*) Seth, come back. Sit down until I have finished. (SETH *returns to chair.*) Now beware of what you do. To-night, I will call upon you at the mill, and bring with me that five thousand. Until that time, promise me that your lips shall be sealed.

SETH. You have my promise.

JACOB. Good. To-night, we will talk this matter over candidly. Why, man, with the amount I shall pay you added to what you already have, you will be independent. Don't crush that independence by returning money to a man who would use it to frustrate my designs.

SETH. Your designs are villainous. You would force a girl to marry you contrary to her wishes. I tell you it is not right. So much innocence should not be joined to such a mountain of guilt. (JACOB *winces.*) Oh, you can wince, Jacob, but I mean it.

JACOB. Bah! you would do the same thing if given an opportunity.

(ELIAS *is seen to appear in archway,* C.)

SETH. Never. Villain though I am, I respect a woman. They are man's helpmeet; and as such should wed a man, and not one whose manhood has been crushed out of him. We are not men, Jacob, we are fiends; and too many such fiends have dragged noble woman down to their same level. Charge me with the whole catalogue of crimes; but don't you dare repeat that I would insult a woman.

ELIAS (*advancing front*). Ye ha' a spark of manhood about ye that I had not dreamed of.

SETH } (*turning upon him in* { The devil!
JACOB } *surprise*). { Curses light on you! why
{ are you here?

ELIAS. I ha' a word t' say t' ye, Jacob, an' I be willin' ye both shall listen. Between the two of you, ye ha' made my life miserable; an' even now ye be not satisfied until ye ha' crushed me into the grave. Ye ha' bound me by an oath, an' I ha' kept it; an' by the keeping of it, ye ha' been saved from the gallows. This, however, has not led ye t' regard me with any favor: for if ye ha' a chance t' bear down upon me, ye do it with all the power ye can command. I ha' but few friends, an' ye be the cause of it; an' the few friends I have ye delight t' torture in a way that makes ye despisable. Ye ha' turned Phillip into the street, an' ye done it out of spite. I had the money t' settle his notes, an' that money was good, an' ye knew it. If ye two stole it, then ye be worse than a Judas: for he hanged himself for his sin, while ye ha' not the kindness t' do it. Now I would ask of ye a

favor; an' if the keepin' of that oath ha' been the saving of
ye, ye will grant it.   Will ye leave Edward unmolested, an'
once more place Phillip Raymond in his old home?

JACOB (*emphatically*).   No; not until he settles his notes,
or that girl becomes my wife.

SETH.   Hold on, Jacob.   A hasty decision is often the
cause of much evil.

JACOB.   Well!

SETH.   The sword of Damocles hangs over us.   You
must remove it.

JACOB.   There is nothing to remove.   If he fails to
settle the notes he must expect to suffer the penalty.   I gave
him the time allotted by law before turning him out of the
house.   Unless he does settle them, he shall never again
return to his old home.

SETH.   If the money should be raised — what then?

JACOB (*aside*).   Curse him! he is determined to work
against me.   (*Aloud.*)   Why, if he raises the money, that
ends it; that is, so far as Raymond is concerned.   As to
this fellow's accomplice, he has meddled too much with my
affairs to receive any leniency whatever.

ELIAS.   He has not meddled with your affairs, Jacob
Johnson, he has not done it.   He has but performed an act
what wus right in the sight of God an' man.   If ye think t'
marry Mabel with the crimes ye ha' committed staining your
character, ye shall be disappointed : for I will work against
it with all the means that lay in my power.

JACOB.   What! would you break your oath?   Beware! or
you shall not be given an opportunity.   Remember, I am
not to be trifled with.

ELIAS.   I ha' no fears for your threats, I be beyond that.
I shall keep the oath I ha' taken as I ha' promised; but if
the worst comes t' the worst, I ha' a way t' reveal it.

JACOB (*startled*).   What mean you?   (SETH *turns and
looks* ELIAS *full in the face.*)

ELIAS.   First, will ye grant me the favors I ha' asked of
ye?

JACOB.   My answer is given.   Only to yourself will I show
the least compassion.   And this, understand me, is not
through fear of any punishment you can inflict.

ELIAS (*forcibly*).   Then, Jacob Johnson, listen t' my

words. Often in the small hours of the night I ha' kept awake, an' studied upon that oath, an' prayed t' God t' show me a way out of it, an' at last my prayer ha' been answered. The language of that oath, an' I ha' not forgotten it, is this: "As God is my witness, I will keep this secret until my dying day." Do ye mark that? "— until my dying day." Now if ye refuse me the favors I ha' asked, I will ha' a dying day, an' it will come sooner than ye expect it; an' when it does come, ye two shall suffer for the crimes ye ha' committed. This be my curse. (*Turns slowly, and exits* C.)

JACOB (*after a pause*). Well!

SETH. Well, Jacob.

JACOB. He dare not do it.

SETH. He will. You must do as he has said.

JACOB. And give up that girl? Never!

SETH. But I say you shall.

JACOB. What!

SETH. My liberty is at stake as well as yours. The vilest worm that crawls will cling to life. So will I. You must come to terms.

JACOB (*aside*). I will pretend to yield. (*Aloud.*) Very well; we will talk it over, to-night.

SETH (*rising*). I tell you, Jacob, we must be cautious. Crime cannot toy with justice no more than fire with powder. You give up the girl, and I will give up the money. Between the two, we can undo one act out of the many we have committed. Think it over. (*Exit* C.)

JACOB (*down* C.). Yes, I'll think it over, and in a way not suited to your taste. To-night I will visit him at his room, and that visit shall be our last. I will drug him with wine, and then rob him, not only of the paper he holds against me, but of that money. Then with coal gas I will asphyxiate that other wretch, after which, I will fire the mill. This will rid me of two enemies at once, and I shall be free. (*Shaking his fist off* C.) Remember, Seth Randolph, that those who plot against Jacob Johnson, will come to grief, as you shall find out to your sorrow.

(*Scene closes in.*)

SCENE II. — *Highway.*

(MABEL *enters from* L.)

MABEL. Oh, what will be the end of all this? Turned into the streets without even a place to lay our heads. The thought is terrible. I care not for myself; but my poor father. Oh, to think that he should be brought to this! (*Looks off* L.) There he comes now, led on by my ever patient mother. In his arms he carries his bible, which he clings to through all his adversities.

(*Slow music.* PHILLIP *enters from* L. *led on by* MRS. RAYMOND.)

PHILLIP (*speaking as he enters*). Theer — theer, Betty, don't be discouraged. The good Lord will guide us through the wilderness like as he did the Israelites of old, if we're not afeerd to trust him. I am not worrit for ourselves — not for ourselves, Betty. I thowt as how this thing might happen, theerfur it comes kiend of nat'ral like to bear it. Mabel, hold this book. (MABEL *takes bible.*) These here knees of mine shakes a-most like poplar leaves in a gale, and I can navigate no furder. Bear a hand, Betty, and help me. (PHILLIP *is assisted to a seat on bank.*) Theer! theer! that's right. Now give me that theer bible.

MRS. R. O Phillip! you will never stand this journey. The shades of night are falling, a storm is approaching, and we have not reached a single house. If obliged to remain out to-night it will be the death of you. (*Lightning and thunder ; distant.*)

MABEL. Surely, mother, some kind neighbors will take us in if we can only reach them. It is only a mile to Lucy's cottage. If we can reach that, I know she will give us shelter.

PHILLIP. The two of you must not worry on my account. I'm a-going to be rested in a minute, and wen I am, I'll journey along furder like a new man. If we reach Lucy's, well and good. If not, we have the happ'ness to know that the Lord is with us.

MRS. R. Well, Phillip, for my part, I feel that the Lord has deserted us.

PHILLIP. Theer, Betty, is wheer you have made a mistake. It is we poor critters who, in our shortsightedness desert the Lord. You remember wen the ship left us in Liverpool — left us a-standing theer on the dock and sailed away widout us — well, the ship went down and was lost, while we what was left on the dock was saved. Theer was a blessing as awaited us as we little dreamed of. Now, wen these here troubles come, and saddens our 'arts, making us rebellious like, sermuch so that we could take the reins out of the Lord's hands to run to our own liking, it is time to stop. In the eend, them theer calamities may be seen to be d'rected to our future happ'ness and welfare. Don't find fault with the ways of the Lord until you know you are wiser than He is.

LUCY (*who has entered from* R.). For the land sakes! has the millerium come, or am I lookin' cross-eyed. (*Looking sharply at* PHILLIP.) I declare! it is Phillip, sure as natur. Has the house burned up, or what on airth is the matter.

MABEL. Mr. Johnson has turned us into the street, Lucy. Even now we are seeking for a place of shelter.

LUCY. You don't say! The old curmudgeon! turned your poor blind father into the streets? I allus did think that Jacob wus sorter perunious, but I never charged him with sech meanness as that. An' you are seekin' for shelter? Land sakes! you jest bundle up an' follow me right back hum.

MRS. R. Will it not be intruding too much upon your generosity? Remember, Lucy, we are without a dollar.

LUCY. Land a massey! what do I keer about money. While I've got a hunk o' pork, an' tu turnips, you're welcome tu 'em, goodness knows! Why, I had jest started for your house. Well, wonders will never cease! The next thing we know, water will run up hill without a hydraulin' ram. Come, Phillip, come tu my house, an' I'll give you as good a cup o' Rapanese tea as you ever tasted. Nuthin like Rapanese or Hysong tea tu quiet the nerves, I kin tell ye.

MRS. R. O Lucy! how can we ever thank you?

LUCY. There! don't mention that agin. Come, Phillip, I'm good on a lift, if I am clumsy. (LUCY *and* MRS. RAYMOND *assist* PHILLIP *to his feet. Lightning and thunder distant.*)

PHILLIP. I told you, Betty, as how summat ud turn up, and theer has even afore I was aweer. If we cannot reward you in this wureld, Lucy, I'm a'most sure you will be rewarded in the next. This here book that I hold has said it, and it has never told a lie.

MRS. R. We will not burden you, only for the night. On the morrow, Mabel and I will seek work, and if we find it, will arrange a place for Phillip.

LUCY. Don't you fret about Phillip. Land sakes! I've got room enough for us all, an' four cats besides. Now you jest follow me, an' I'll take you hum in half a jiffy. (*All exeunt* R. PHILLIP *assisted by* LUCY *and* MRS. RAYMOND.)

SCENE III. — *Room in* LUCY'S *house. Practical door* R. C. *Window* L. C. *Table near* R. I E. *Chairs, etc. Furniture plain. Lightning and thunder should be continued through the scene, gradually growing nearer. Time, evening.*

(*Enter* LUCY, MR. *and* MRS. RAYMOND *and* MABEL, R. C.)

LUCY. Now jest make yourselves right tu hum. Phillip, you sot down here. (*Leads* PHILLIP *to seat down stage*, L.) There! now I'll jest take your things, an' then I'll fix that Rapanese tea quicker'n a cat kin jump. You see, we don't know when we're apt tu be tooken with sickness, so I allus keeps a kettle o' hot water ready for use. (*Takes things.*) I'll be back'n less'n half a minit. (*Exit* L. I E.)

MRS. R. (*seating herself near* PHILLIP). Good old soul! There is nothing in the house too good for the needy traveler who comes under her sheltering care. Would that the world contained more just such people. (*Lightning and thunder; distant.*)

MABEL. She is, indeed, kind. And how thankful we should be that we reached here before the storm that is approaching had overtaken us. I shudder even now to think of our being exposed to the warring elements. (*Crosses to window.*)

PHILLIP. Theer is a way as is always provided, my child, wen we can master the patience to wait. I had no fears for myself; not for myself as much as for the two of you. I could brave the storm as is a-coming, brave it a'most **cheerful** like, could the sight on'y touch Jacob's 'art and make him feel responsible. But the man as has no 'art, has no sense of responsibility; and that are the trouble with Jacob.

MRS. R. Sometime he may be consumed in the fire of his own kindling; and it may overtake him sooner than he expects it.

PHILLIP. No man can escape the vengeance of the Lord. Bide your time — bide your time, Betty. Why, crippled and sightless as I appear — and I am both, I am sorry to say — I would not change places with that theer Jacob for all his wealth and position. Even the thowt as how such a thing could happen, wownds my 'art, and makes me blush for my manhood.

LUCY (*outside*). Scat! scat! I say. I never saw a cat that wasn't allus a trianglin' under a body's feet. (*Enters* L. 1 E.). Land a massey! I nearly upsot the hull of this tea on the floor. (*Crosses to* PHILLIP.) Now, Phillip, you drink this, an' if it don't recreate your spirits like a glass of Bogun whiskey, I'll spin you a skein o' yarn for nuthin'. The rest of us will drink ours in t'other room. (*Gives cup and saucer to* PHILLIP.)

PHILLIP. Lucy, theer are names as this world will remember long after yours is forgotten; but while the next world may not contain of them so much as a scratch, yours will shine out emblazoned with gold. I hope as how this will be the case.

LUCY. Land sakes! how much like Uriah you du talk. You used tu know Uriah afore you wus tooken with blindness. Well, he argefied so much on the scrip'ters, an' how people should conductor themselves in this world, an' all that sort o' thing, that I used tu think he wus out of his head. Poor man! he's dead, though, an' here I am, a lone widder, a-tryin' tu keep soul an' body together.

MABEL (*at window*). Mercy! how dark it grows. (*Flash of lightning.*) And the storm — how swiftly it approaches.

MRS. R. Now that we are sheltered from its fury we can regard it without alarm; but to think how narrowly we escaped from facing it — even now it makes me shudder.

LUCY. Land sakes! let the storm alone. Uriah used tu say that the more we medicated over troubles, the larger they grew. I allow its about so. I'll jest light a candle an' scatter 'em out along with the shaders. (*Exit* L. 1 E.)

PHILLIP. Theer are wisdom in her words — theer are wisdom in her words. Now, Betty, I have a mind to rest if as how theer is a place to put me.

MRS. R. Lucy is coming now. We will see that you are made as comfortable as possible.

LUCY (*enters* L. 1 E. *with lighted candle. When convenient, this candle should be extremely large*). There! I've got this candle lit at last. It isn't as purty as some, but I reckon there are qualities about it that will last. You see, the taller overrun, so I put the balance into this. I ain't so much on eteket as on sober reality, I kin tell ye. (*Sets candle on table.*)

MRS. R. When convenient, Lucy, you may show Phillip to his room. The excitement of the day, and the fatigue derived from walking, have greatly unnerved him. I will go with you.

LUCY. Gracious! why didn't I think of that afore. Here — I'll take that cup an' saucer. (*Takes cup and saucer.*) Now jest follow me, an' I'll show you the best room in the house.

PHILLIP (*rising from chair assisted by* MRS. RAYMOND). The bible says, "Cast thy bread upon the waters, and it will return to you after many days." Well, I counsels as how you will be rewarded for this here kindness, Lucy, and it may overtake you long afore you are aweer.

LUCY. Land sakes! I hope so. If there's anything I dislike, it is tu wait for things that's a-goin' tu du me any good. (*Exit* L. 1 E., *followed by* MR. *and* MRS. RAYMOND.)

MABEL (*at window*). I love to watch the storm! One flash succeeds another in quick succession, and fills me with awe. In it I behold a power over which we have no control. (*Turns from window.*) O Edward! Edward! How cruelly we were torn apart! Even now you are in hiding for a crime you could not possibly have committed. Some one is guilty of this, and would to Heaven they could be made to suffer. Hark! some one approaches! Who can have wandered here in the face of such a storm.

SAMBO (*rushing in from* R. C.). Lor a-mighty! dis yer chile am frightened mos' to death. Dar's de tarrinest storm a-comin', and I'se gwine to go home right in the face of it.

MABEL. Why, what brings you here?

SAMBO. Fotched a letter to yer, Missey Mabel — fotched it from Mas'r Johnson. Lor a-mighty! I'se done trabbeled de whole country ober — thought I should nebber find you, sure. Here's de letter, Missey Mabel; hope dar's nuffin in it to harrer your feelings. (*Gives letter.*)

MABEL (*taking letter*). A letter for me? And from Jacob? (*Aside.*) How my heart beats! (*Opens letter.*) I tremble to read the contents. (*Reads.*)

"To Miss Raymond:

Unless you call upon me to-morrow with a satisfactory answer, your father will be arrested for a forgery committed against me in the past, as also will that upstart, Edward, for passing counterfeit money. Accept my hand, and all will be dropped.

JACOB."

O Heaven! the blow has fallen. What shall I do! It must — yes, it shall be done. (*To* SAMBO.) Run — run to your master. Tell him I will be there — that I will see him in the morning as early as possible.

SAMBO. I'll tole him — I'll tole him, Missey Mabel. 'Spec's dat man am up to some more of his deviltry. (*Starts off.*) Doan know what am de trubble wid Mas'r Johnson — keeps dis chile running wid letters de whole time lately. (*Lightning and thunder.*) For de Lord's sake! if dis chile doan hurry he will get cotched in the hurryclone sure. (*Runs out* R. C.)

MABEL. The die is cast. I am destined to become the bride of a man I utterly loathe. My poor father must not know of this; only to my mother will I reveal the secret. Oh, why are we so afflicted when there are so many around us who are happy.

MRS. R. (*enters* L. I. E.). Did I not hear some one enter the room? (*Perceives that Mabel is agitated.*) Why, my child, what is the matter?

MABEL. O mother! mother! how can I ever tell you? Read this — it will explain all. (*Gives letter.*)

MRS. R. (*reads letter*). Oh, the villain! We are lost! lost! (*Sinks into chair*, C.)

MABEL. No. mother, no. I will save you, though it breaks my heart in doing it. I will accept his offer.

MRS. R. You — you, Mabel? Impossible! you know not what you say.

MABEL. Mother, listen to me. Unless I marry Jacob, father is ruined — Edward is ruined. If my poor hand can save them, consent that I shall make the sacrifice.

MRS. R. But your father, Mabel.

MABEL. He must not know it. Only yourself shall enter into the secret. If father is arrested, and sent to prison, he will surely die. Mother, you must consent.

MRS. R. Oh, my child! I dare not consent to what I know will be the ruin of your life. Act your own judgment, Mabel, and may God direct you in the right course.

MABEL. Then mother, though it breaks my heart in doing it, I will marry Jacob Johnson, (*Sinks at her mother's feet, and buries her face in her lap.*)

SCENE IV. *Highway. Night. Storm still continued.*

JACOB (*enters*). The night is as favorable as I could wish. The wind from the advancing storm will fan the flames, and the rain will entirely obliterate my footprints from the soil. It was on such a night that — bah! why will the scenes of that night for ever rise up before me. Do what I will, I cannot efface the picture of that murdered man from my memory. Well, no more of this! Such thoughts will make a coward of me; and if I ever needed courage, it is in the job I have before me. It is evident that those men must be disposed of, or I am ruined. Ruined? Curse them! they shall never take from me that wealth which my scheming has gathered together. These men disposed of, the power to put Phillip and that young upstart in jail, and that girl is completely in my power. Ha! ha! when kindness fails, then force must be resorted to, is the rule I work by. (*Exit* L.)

SCENE V. — *Interior of mill, same as in Act 2., Scene 1. Night. Lightning and thunder, wind and rain. Lighted candle in each room.* SETH *discovered in room to* L. *He is sitting on cot with his head resting upon his hands as if despondent.* ELIAS *and* EDWARD *discovered in room to* R. ELIAS *sits upon side of cot.* EDWARD *in chair. Music at rise of curtain.*

EDWARD. Say, Elias, this thing is about played. Lodging in a wheel pit is worse than joining the nomads. Besides, it isn't half so pleasant. I'm going to take my bundle and emigrate.

ELIAS. Ye must ha' patience, Edward. So far ye be not mistrusted of hiding here; not even by the occupant of the adjoining room. I ha' reason t' think he be out tonight, so ye can talk with freedom. Ha' patience for a little longer, an' ye will not regret it.

EDW. Well, haven't I had patience. I've hung in that water-soaked hole until I'm bleached out whiter than a winter ermine. Who has visited me? Nothing but rats. Now what are the presence of rodents compared to the presence of the woman you love.

ELIAS. Ha' patience for a little, Edward, an' ye shall see her. Even now she may not be so well situated as yourself.

EDW. What do you mean by that?

ELIAS. I tell ye, Edward, that the blow Phillip expected has fallen. To-day he has been turned into the streets. Even now they may be exposed t' the storm that ye hear approaching.

EDW. (*jumping to his feet*). Curse of Minerva! you don't mean it. Give me my hat! I'm out of here quicker than a streak of chain lightning. (*Starts for door.*)

ELIAS (*rising and catching hold of his arm*). Ye must not go, Edward. Come back, an' I will give ye an explanation.

EDW. What! and leave Mabel out in the storm? What do you take me for? I'll find her a shelter, and give that Jacob the St. Vitus dance, or I'm not a Le Roy. Let go of my arm.

ELIAS (*dragging him back*). Edward, ye must listen t' reason. Sit down until I ha' finished talking t' ye. (EDWARD *resists.*) Sit down, I tell ye. (*Forces him into chair.*) Why, man, ye ha' not the sense o' the girl that ye love. Think ye I would leave them t' battle the gale? Ye ha' no common sense, man.

EDW. But you say that, even now they might be exposed to the storm.

ELIAS. I said that t' show ye how others could be as bad

off as yourself. Now if ye ha' a mind t' listen, I will explain. (*Sits on side of couch.*) If possible Mabel was t'
reach Lucy's cottage with her parents; an' she had half of
the day in which t' do it. If she failed, I was t' be notified.
As I ha' not been notified, I ha' reasons t' feel that they be
safe.

EDW. Well, that's a relief; but that hound of a Jacob —
what about him? Blast it! I could make a sieve of him in
just about five minutes. I believe him capable of anything —
murder even, if given an opportunity.

ELIAS (*agitated*). Hush! hush! Edward; ye ha' not a
right t' say that. Ye can call call him a bad man — a very
bad man; but ye ha' no right t' say he would murder. Ye
do not know it.

EDW. Well, a murder has been committed in these parts,
and you know who done it. Now I'll bet a dollar —

ELIAS (*rising*). Edward, ye had better go into hiding.
I would not have you found out by the man of the next
room. (*Goes and opens trap.*) The storm be on the increase, and will send him in.

EDW. Let him come. Blast him! I believe it was he
who stole that money. Oh, I could annihilate him and
everybody else. (*Springing to his feet.*) I'm a regular
Hercules boiling for a fight.

ELIAS. Ye may feel like a Hercules, Edward, but ye ha'
not the looks of one. Come! ye had better go below.

EDW. Well, just as you say. (*Descending trap.*) Hang
it! I don't like being a prisoner. How long has this thing
got to last?

ELIAS. Not for long, Edward. The day be not far distant when ye shall be free. I ha' a way t' do it that ye ha'
not dreamed of.

EDW. Thank the Lord for that. Well, if you hear a
howl in the night, you may know I've struck a rat. Hurry
matters along, because the quarters I occupy are worse than
a spare bedroom in winter. (*Disappears.*)

ELIAS (*closing trap*). Ye little know, Edward, of the
sacrifice I shall make, ye little know it. (*Advancing front.
Lightning and thunder.*) There be a terrible storm out o'
doors, an' it be a fit companion t' the fiercer storm within
my heart. Alas! there be nothing left for me but t' die; an'

t' accomplish it, I ha' the means in this bottle. (*Takes phial from his pocket. Holds it up and looks at it.*) To-morrow, I will return my life t' the God who gave it, an' when dying, will reveal the secret that has preyed upon my mind for years. If it be a sin, then may the Lord forgive me: for I take my life for the purpose of doing good. (*Returns phial to his pocket.*) Now for the last time I will seek my couch; an' if I sleep, it will be my last but one upon earth. (*Extinguishes candle.*) God only knows the agony I suffer; an' if He be a just God, He will save me from this terrible doom. (*Throws himself upon couch. Storm grows nearer.*)

(*During the last of* ELIAS'S *soliloquy,* SETH *arouses himself, and looks around as if dazed. Then he rises, and mechanically approaches front, pauses, and stares at the floor like one in deep meditation. As* ELIAS *seeks his couch,* SETH *slowly speaks.*)

SETH. There may be no direct communication between this world and the next; but if a muffled sentence don't reach us once in a while from that unseen country, then I'm a liar. Something to-night whispers to me of danger; and I can catch the word, "danger! danger! danger!" just as plain as I can catch the sound of the wind there on the outside. If it isn't some spirit whispering in my ears, then what is it? Jacob is overdue. Curse it! I put no more confidence in that man than I do in myself; or half as much. Without confidence the heart is weak; therefore, to insure the safety of my valuables, I had better hide them. (*Takes paper and wallet from his pocket. Removes money and returns wallet back again. Looks at paper.*) This paper is Jacob's confession to that murder; and while I hold it, he is in my power. Once lost, and my game is up. (*Hides paper and money under head of cot.*) Hark! he comes. It will not do to find me here. (*Fixes cot, crosses room, and seats himself opposite stand as* JACOB *enters* C. L.)

JACOB (*coming down*). Seth?

SETH. Jacob!

JACOB. I have arrived.

SETH. So I perceive. I was aware of the close proximity of some evil spirit five minutes ago. Please be seated.

JACOB (*seating himself on cot*). I have come to bring you

that five thousand as I agreed. · It is best that two men situated as we are should be on friendly terms. We may need each other's assistance.

SETH. True! I had not thought of that. Assistance in the hour of trouble is a godsend. And such assistance! Well, where's the check?

JACOB. Here it is. (*Producing check.*) Examine it closely, and see if it is all right. (*Gives check; aside.*) It is only loaned for a few hours.

SETH (*examining check*). Five thousand dollars! Well, that means Paris and the old continent. The signature is a little shaky, but never mind. (*Puts check in his pocket.*) Jacob?

JACOB. Well!

SETH. Let us shake. (*They shake hands.*) Such friendship as yours is without a parallel. How can I ever reward you for this great sacrifice upon your wealth.

JACOB. It is nothing. Assist me to wed that girl, and it shall be doubled. You made one grand stroke when you stole that money. (*Ironically.*) For me it was the grandest stroke you ever made.

SETH (*sarcastically*). Yes, it was a beautiful stroke; a most excellent stroke. Why, it placed in my pocket over five thousand dollars. Besides, it ruined a whole family, shattered the prospects of a loving couple, and made me hate myself. Oh, that was a delightful stroke, Jacob.

JACOB. Bah! haven't you recovered from your weakness of to-day? Why, man, you are growing penitent. Come! let us drink. (*Takes bottle and glass from pocket.*)

SETH. Now, Jacob, you have touched a tender chord. No man understands the little weaknesses of my heart like yourself. However, I must refuse. ·

JACOB. Refuse? What! Seth Randolph refuse a drink! Now do I believe in your repentance?

SETH (*rising to his feet and speaking forcibly*). Hark'ee, Jacob, and I'll give you a lesson in Temperance. I learned to drink in early youth. It became a power over which I had no control. It lured me to the gambling table. It led me to squander my inheritance, and sink my father in bankruptcy. Once, when heated with wine, and half crazed, I struck my mother to the earth for reproving me for my conduct. From that moment no word ever issued from her lips, and she went to the grave, where she was soon after joined by my father. Then I fled — fled from that home which gave me birth. I came to you. I placed myself under your fostering care. And such care! How like a shepherd you have watched over me, Jacob. To you I owe my first knowledge of crime. With you am I guilty of murder. Now, you ask me to drink. Why? Not out of friendship, — oh, no! Oh! I know you, Jacob, and that knowledge leads me to be wary.

JACOB (*unmoved*). Seth, this is Madeira, your favorite drink. (*Holding up bottle.*)

SETH (*forcibly*). Well, what is Madeira when poisoned.

JACOB. Poisoned? Why, man, what do you mean? What reason have I for putting you out of the way?

SETH. Because, I am an obstacle in your path. You tried it once and failed. Since then I have been cautious.

JACOB. Seth, you are mad. Don't judge me by the past. To-night, I come to you as a friend; and have proved it, by giving you that check. Here — I will drink first to convince you that this wine is all right. (*Fills glass and drinks.*)

(SETH *approaches front. As he does so,* JACOB *quickly drops powder into tumbler.*)

SETH (*aside*). Am I mistaken? How can he poison that which he drinks himself. These parched lips crave the drink that he offers, and yet, something in here whispers not to touch it. If I now refuse, he will call me a coward; and that I can never stand. (*Aloud.*) Jacob?

JACOB. Well!

SETH. Fill up that glass. (JACOB *fills glass.*) Give it to me. (*Takes glass.*) Now you say this wine is all right?

JACOB. How can it be otherwise when I have drank of it myself?

SETH. Stranger miracles than that have happened, even in the nineteenth century. (*Holding up glass and looking into it.*) Beware of the serpent in the glass! (*Raises glass to his lips, pauses, then looks sharply at* JACOB.) Jacob, if you are deceiving me, you had better pause. I shall live long enough to tear you limb from limb.

JACOB (*slightly agitated*). The wine is all right.

SETH. Very well. (*Lifting glass.*) Then here is luck to

one or both of us. (*Drinks half of glass, suddenly stops, looks into tumbler, then at* JACOB, *and then hurls glass upon the floor.*)   Curse you! you have played me false.

JACOB (*retreating*).   You are mistaken.   The wine was all right, I tell you.

SETH.   You lie.   The taste was peculiar.   Even now I can feel it permeating through every fiber of my system. Hell furies seize! you shall suffer for this. (*Staggers down front, draws knife, and turns back.   Lightning and heavy thunder.   Music.*)

JACOB (*draws revolver and retreats down* C.).   Back! back! I say.   Approach me at your peril.

SETH.   With death staring me in the face, I know no peril.   Curse you! we will die together. (*Starts forward again — staggers.* JACOB *avoids and runs down front.*) You shall never escape me! I tell you, you shall not! (*Turns, reels forward, striking wildly with knife.* JACOB *again avoids him and runs down stage.*)   O God! am I too late? Fool! fool that I was to trust you! (*Makes one more effort to rush forward, suddenly stops, drops knife, and clasps his hands to his head.*)   Ha! my brain!   My eyes grow dim!   Oh, I am lost! lost! (*Staggers back and falls heavily to the floor.* JACOB *stands in background, with drawn revolver, watching him.   At last he approaches, takes him by the shoulder and shakes him.*)

JACOB.   He is safe enough for the present.   I perceived his condition, or would have shot him down like a dog. Now for the check and the paper he holds against me. *Takes check from pocket.*)   Here is the check.   Fool! did he think I would give him that money? (*Returns check to his own pocket and then continues search.*)   Where can he have placed that paper? (*Finds wallet.*)   Ah! here it is. (*Opens wallet.*) Curse it! the wallet is empty.   Never mind; I can wait no longer.   Fire will consume the paper, and the money I can do without. (*Throws wallet upon stand.*)   Now for fixing that idiot in the next room, and then to fire the mill. (*Goes out* L. C. *and returns with pan of coal.*)   The coal is as I left it and well on fire.   Once the room is filled with gas, and he is safe. (*Removes board from centre partition, and cautiously inserts pan into next room.*)   There! nothing could work more satisfactory.   To fire the mill is easy.   In the room

below are a lot of rags and shavings which will easily ignite.
I will set them on fire and then — peace be to their ashes.
(*Goes to center of room, turns, looks carefully around, then
goes out* C. L. *Lightning and thunder, wind and rain.*) *

(*Pause. Music through rest of scene. Red lights which
gradually increase in brilliancy off* R. *and* L. *Fire and smoke
gradually seen through different parts of the stage. Heavy
fire and smoke under trap to be seen when trap is open.
Time must be allowed to make the scene appear natural. At
last* SETH *is seen to slowly move. Then, with apparent exertion, he sits upright and looks wildly around. Clasping
his hands to his forehead, he utters a cry, and staggers to
his feet.*)

SETH.   O Heavens! am I asleep? Do I dream? Oh! it
comes to me now. That accursed wine! Fool that I was
to touch it! Ha! what means this? The room on fire?
My God! 'tis too true. Curses light on that fiend, this is
his work! (*Staggers to cot.*) I must save that paper.
Without it my hold upon that man is lost. (*Takes articles
from cot, and puts them in his pocket.*) Now for revenge on
that Devil in human shape. (*Runs to door which he finds
locked.*) What! locked in? Caged here like a dog to perish?
It must not — shall not be! (*Rushes down* C. *Recollects himself.*) Hold, Seth. Brace up and be a man. Do away with this
cowardice. He whom you have wronged is doubtless in like
danger. You must save him! Save him, if you perish in the
attempt. (*Crosses to partition, tears out boards, and crawls
into room. Perceiving the pan of coal, he picks it up and
hurls it through window, breaking glass.*) There, that is disposed of. Now to save the man I have wronged. (*Shaking
ELIAS.*) Rouse up here or you are lost! (*Dragging him
from cot.*) Wake up, my friend, or your doom is sealed.

ELIAS (*rousing himself and perceiving* SETH). You be
here? Ha' ye the wickedness t' murder me?

SETH.   I would save you. Look! we are surrounded by
fire. Come! come with me. (*Starting with him toward
door.*)

ELIAS (*holding back*). No — no; I be not going! I —

* For description of fire scene, see page 3.

I — Edward! he be beneath the trap. Leave me, and save him. O Heavens! I — I choke — (*Falls heavily upon floor.*)

SETH. A man below? I'll save them both or perish! (*Drags* ELIAS *to door which he finds locked.*) This locked? Oh, for the strength of a giant! (*Hurls himself against door which gives way.*) There! (*Drags* ELIAS *to the outside, then returns.*) Now for the man in the room beneath. My brain is on fire; but I must not — will not fail. (*Lifts trap. As he does so, fire and smoke issue through opening.* SETH *pauses a moment, then dashes in.*)

EDW. (*outside*). What ! trying to save me? Blast it! I ain't there! I doubted your word and started after Mabel. Discovering the mill on fire, I turned back. Come! let's to the rescue.

ELIAS (*enters* C. D. *followed by* EDWARD). Ye go back, Edward, ye go back. I ha' nothing t' lose if I perish. Ye go back. (*Descends trap.*)

EDW. Not while a man is in danger. If he risked his life for me, it is right I should risk mine for him. (*Follows* ELIAS. *Music. They soon emerge dragging the form of* SETH. *His clothes are on fire, and his face blackened with smoke.*) I'm afraid we're too late. He's a dead man.

ELIAS. It has that appearence. We ha' not a moment t' lose. (*They start with* SETH *toward door.*)

SETH (*with effort*). Wait! wait but a moment! (*Turns so as to face audience.*) Let — let me speak! J-Jacob — O God! he — Jacob, he done this — he — he — (*Falls back into their arms.*)

CURTAIN.

ACT IV.

SCENE I.—*Room in Lucy's house, same as in Act 3, Scene 3. Time, morning. Large sun bonnet and shawl on table. As curtain rises, Lucy and Mabel are discovered.*

LUCY (*assisting* MABEL). Well, I s'pose if you must go, you must. Of course you know your own business best, though there's a heap o' people as don't. How long will it be afore you'll return?

MABEL. If nothing happens, dear Lucy, I shall be here to dine with you. Should I be detained you must not wait for me. Some matters I have to adjust may keep me unavoidably delayed.

LUCY. Land sakes! don't let any orinary matters rob you of your dinner. Uriah used tu say, that, tu work on an empty stomach, wus next thing tu visiting an overtaken; an' Uriah used tu hit things about correct. Why, I'm going tu have frickerseed chicken for dinner, with injin molasses for a side dish; an' I wouldn't have you miss it for a pewter button.

MABEL. I will endeavor, if possible. not to disappoint you. (*Going to door.*) Tell mother I started somewhat earlier than I intended, and thought best not to disturb her. If nothing prevents, I shall be here by twelve. (*Exit* C. R.)

LUCY (*at door*). Well, I shall look for you with all the eyes I've got. (*Speaking off.*) When you cross over the hill, jest look in the direction of your father's mill. I saw a big light in that direction last night, an' ten to one if Elias hain't sot it on fire. (*Closes door and comes down front.*) It is cu'rus how Phillip lets every straggler inter that mill, jest because there happens tu be a couple of empty rooms. Tu hear any day that it had burned down wouldn't surprise me in the least. (*Goes to table and puts on sun bonnet and shawl.*) Kinder cu'rus what Mabel is after on sech a mornin' as this. Why, the road is full of gullets from last night's rain. She seem agitated, tu. Likely as not she has gone over tu intercreed with Jacob; an' poor consolation she will get. (*Noticing that she has put on things.*) Goodness gracious! what hev I got these things on for? I ain't a-goin' anywheres. (*Takes off bonnet and shawl and throws them on table.*) I du believe I'm growing more an' more absent minded every day. Next thing I know, I shall be mistakin' some man for my departed Uriah. Well, I can hear Phillip, so I reckon I had better fix up things. (*Arranges chairs, etc.*)

(PHILLIP, *carrying bible, enters* L. I. E. *assisted by* MRS. RAYMOND.

PHILLIP. You say as how Mabel has left her room. Now wot I say is, if Mabel has left her room, wheer can the child have gone?

MRS. R. (*assisting him to chair*). I think, Phillip, that she is not far away. Trouble for the past few days, may have unsettled her nerves. No doubt she has gone out for a morning walk from which she will soon return.

LUCY. Land a massey! let the child alone. Airly mornin' walks is what throws the blood into the cheeks; an' goodness knows she needs it at present. She said she had some business, or suthin', tu attend tu; but if possible, would be back by twelve. I hope she will, for if she don't, that frickerseed chicken will be cold as a dog's nose in January. She et a lunch afore she started, so I reckon she won't starve.

PHILLIP (*agitated*). You see as to how it is, Betty. The child had business afore her. It is not for long she would walk on a morning like this, for it is wet and windy. The child had business that took her away. On'y give me the nature of that business afore my suspicions lead me astray.

MRS. R. Phillip, I think you are borrowing unnecessary trouble. Whatever business Mabel may have before her, believe me, it is for our benefit.

PHILLIP. Theer it is again. I tell you, Betty, theer is that underlying your words as befogs them. I am not to be deceived. I have the sense of understanding, and this here blindness of mine has made it sharp, and easy to penetrate the truth. You are prevaricating with me, as I am well aweer; and I have the boldness to say, and with good reason, too, as how it is not right. Tell me, Betty, if the nature of Mabel's business has anything to do with that theer Jacob?

MRS. R. Oh, Phillip, how should I know! Do not compel me to say that which I shall be sorry for — oh, do not!

PHILLIP Sorry for? Are you that sorry, that you fear to speak the truth? I have not forgotten the words of that child — not as I heerd them from her own lips. I remember as how she said — and I heerd her say it, you understand — heerd her say as how she would marry Jacob, and save her father. Now, Betty, is it come to pass that she is giving herself to that theer snake to save us?

MRS. R. (*bursting into tears*). O Phillip! Phillip!

LUCY. Land a massey! you don't think Mabel would marry Jacob, do ye? I as soon think of her marrying an ooring owtang without any teeth. You let Mabel alone for that.

PHILLIP. Mabel has a self-sacrificing disposition. She loves her old blind father — God bless her 'art for it! and she would sacrifice herself to save him. I know wot that theer Jacob is after. I remember as how, to please him, I put my name upon paper — upon a paper I didn't understand. For you know, Betty, I was ignorant as to business affairs, and at the time was half blind; and the signing of that paper was one of my greatest weaknesses. Well, of a suddint, and it was like as a shock to me, he held up that paper, and called it a forgery. Then, to save the exposure as would nat'rally follow, I — fool that I was — mortgaged him my property, and made myself his pris'ner. Now he wants my Mabel. Because he can't have her, and I can't pay the debts as I never owed, it comes nat'ral to turn us into the street. Is it not likewise nat'ral to punish me for that theer crime, unless Mabel sacrifices herself to gratify his wishes?

MRS. R. O Phillip! let Mabel explain this matter to you as she will. Why will you force me to speak when you know it is breaking my heart?

PHILLIP. Because it is right. What! would you trample your own flesh and blood in the dust for the sake of walking upon roses? Out upon you for the dolt that you are! (*Attempting to rise.*) Help me to my feet.

MRS. R. Why, Phillip, what would you do?

PHILLIP. I'm a-going to find Mabel and bring her back. I'm a-going to hear from her own lips whether the suspicions

I have against her have any foundation or not. I tell you I'm a-going to find out. (*Struggling to rise.*)

MRS. R. (*forcing him back into chair*). Wait, Phillip, and I will tell you all. It is true she has gone to Jacob's. O Phillip! he wrote her a letter stating if she didn't marry him, he would arrest you for forgery, and Edward for passing counterfeit money. She has gone to give him her hand to save Edward and you.

LUCY. Land a massey! who ever heard the beat.

PHILLIP. I thowt it! I thowt it! I tell you. (*Struggling to his feet.*) Give me my hat and lead the way.

MRS. R. Where would you go?

PHILLIP. I'm a-going to that theer Jacob's and meet him face to face. I can't see him with that ugly visage of his; but I can hear him talk, which is quite enough. I'm a-going to make him retract that promise — if I thowt as how Mabel had given it — or I'll knock him down, if it takes this here bible to do it.

MRS. R. (*trying to keep him back*). Phillip, you have not the strength. The distance is altogether too great.

PHILLIP. Strength? I'm all strength. I feel like as how my muscles had turned to iron. I could walk miles — miles, I tell you, before she should wed that theer viper as I knows him to be. Give me my hat. (*Groping wildly around.*) Come! is there no one to help me find my Mabel?

LUCY. Goodness gracious! I'll help ye if I die a widder in doing it. Here — here's your hat. (*Gets his hat and puts it upon his head.*) There now, Betty and I will lead you, an' it won't be no fault of ourn if you don't reach Jacob's afore you know it. That frickerseed chicken can have a postponement. (*They put on things.*)

MRS. R. O Phillip! what will be the end of all this?

PHILLIP. The end, as I knows it, is at that theer Jacob's; and theer it is I'm a-going to go. Come, Betty, bear a hand. Lead the way, and I'll follow you with the strength of a giant. (*They exeunt R. C. door.*)

SCENE II. — *A wood; or, when convenient, interior of shed joining* RAYMOND'S *house.* EDWARD *and* SAMBO *enter from* L. *supporting* SETH RANDOLPH.

SETH. (*slowly, and with much exertion*). It is no use, friends. The days of Seth Randolph are numbered. The

fire I inhaled has done it. I — I had hoped to have reached
th:.t sleuth-hound of a Jacob; but it is too late. Lay me
down, please. I — I have something to say. Something I
must reveal to you before it is too late. (*They place him* C.
of stage back. EDWARD *supports his head.* SAMBO *remains
standing* R.) There! that will do.

EDWARD. Are you comfortable, friend?

SETH. Yes, comfortable as can be expected, if dying is
considered a comfort. (*Looking around.*) Where is the
other?

EDW. If you mean Elias, he has gone to Jacob's.

SAMBO. I comed for him, sah. Dar's trubble at Mas'r
Johnson's — debbil to pay dar, sure. He sent fo' Mabel,
sah. I tooked de letter myself — tooked it right in de face
of de hurryclone. Lor a-mighty! but I was a drownded
nigger, I kin tole yer. Mabel, she comed over dis mornin'
— comed over from Missey Lucy's. I met her down dar by
de ole mill. Why, sah, when she see'd that de ole mill
wasn't dar, she cried, sah, cried like as if her heart would
break. Well, she went over to Mas'r Johnson's, wid me behind her, and on de way, she said, kind of suddin' like, she
wished she was dead. I heard her say it, sah. So 'spectin'
dar was something wrong, I comed and tole Mas'r Elias.
Dat Elias — why, he jess jumped up and started as if de
debbil was after him.

EDW. You see, this Jacob is determined to force Mabel
into a marriage with himself. Elias has gone to upset it
while I watch over you.

SETH. And what a wretch do you watch over. Are you
aware, friend, that you attend a man who has helped to
make all this mischief?

EDW. Well, I had an inkling in that direction. However, this is no time for reproaches. If I can assist you, I
am willing to do it.

SAMBO. I'se of de same mind, Mas'r Somebody.

SETH. A warm heart can beat beneath a black skin.
Yes, you both can assist me. First, open my coat and
remove a wallet you will find in one of the pockets. (ED-
WARD *removes wallet.*) Now, inside of my vest, you will
find a paper. Remove that, please. (EDWARD *removes
paper.*) Thanks now, my black friend, draw closer to me,
and listen to my words.

SAMBO (*sitting close to* SETH, R.). I'se here, sah.

SETH. Very well. Let what I say be indelibly stamped upon your memory. Five years ago, a murder was committed in this town. One there was who witnessed the deed. In order not to share a similar fate, he took upon himself an oath not to reveal it. That oath, through all adversities, he has kept until the present day. You remember him well.

EDW. Yes — Elias. Heavens! that oath has been the ruin of his life.

SETH. It has; and the ones who administered it are guilty of the deed. Now, for aught the public know, the perpetrators of that crime have dwelt in their very midst; and suspicion has diverted first upon one and then upon another. This Elias, so I have learned, told of the murder at the time, and where the body could be found; beyond this, he would not go. Now, friends, I will finish the story. I am partner in crime to the murder of that man. The one who struck the blow, however, was Jacob Johnson.

SAMBO (*holding up his hands in horror*). Lor a-mighty!

EDW. I am not surprised. Go on.

SETH. Gentlemen, with me, and as a dying man I say it, that murder was unintentional. Not one dollar of the money would I touch. After compelling Jacob to admit in writing that he committed the deed, I took the paper, and fled the country. In time I became one of a band of counterfeiters. At last, I returned, bringing money of our own workmanship with me. I took a room in the mill. One night I listened to your conversation with Elias, and learned of the money beneath the trap. I stole it with the result as you have seen. If you will open that wallet, you will find that money, every dollar of it, I wish to return it to its lawful owner. As you were the one to use it, I confide it to your care. Do with it as you think best.

EDW. I will see that Elias has the money. Have you anything further to offer?

SETH (*after a pause*). Only this. That paper is the confession to that murder. Take it, and bring Jacob to justice. As for myself, I am beyond the reach of the law. My life is swiftly ebbing out as I can feel at the present moment. All I ask is, that you will bury me decently. Place me where the birds can sing over me, and where streaks of sun-shine can reach my grave. Leave no stone to mark where I sleep, or — or mention my name. I was not fit to live, and am not fit to be remembered when dead.

EDW. And is this all?

SETH (*slowly and with difficulty*). No; one thing more. There is a locket around my neck. In one side is a likeness of the only woman I ever loved. The other side contains the likeness of my mother. Do not remove the locket, please, or the picture. I — I would have them remain with me until — until — eternity. (*His head slowly sinks upon* EDWARD'S *shoulder*.)

EDW. Believe me, sir, your wish shall be attended to. Is there anything further we can do for you? You may be thirsty; if so, we will procure water. (*Pause.*) Are you more comfortable, friend? (*Pause.*) Have you any further remarks you would like to make? (*Pause. Not answering,* EDWARD *looks into his face and finds him dead.*) Heavens! he is dead.

SAMBO (*jumping to his feet*). Dead? Mas'r Somebody dead?

EDW. Yes, Sambo, he has dropped to sleep in death without a struggle. It is better that it so should be. Let us carry the body to some shelter, procure an officer, and hasten to the house of Jacob at once.

SAMBO. I'se ready, sah. Lor a-mighty! to tink of dis yer chile living at Mas'r Johnson's all dese years widout being murdered. Why, it jess takes away my breff. I'se done living dar now, sah, done fo' sure.

EDW. Well, let us be off. Assist me to remove the body. (EDWARD *lifts at head*, SAMBO *at feet*.)

SAMBO. I'se wid you, sah. Mighty ticklish job, dis! (*Going off.*) Lord! what a narrow escape dis yer chile has had. (*They go off* L. I E. *with body*.)

(*Music*.)

SCENE III. — *Room in* JACOB'S *house, same as in Act I., and Act II. As scene opens,* JACOB *is discovered pacing floor*.

JACOB. As yet, I have heard nothing relating to those who occupied the mill. If they escaped, I should have

heard of it before this. The night was so extremely stormy,
and the building in a spot so secluded, that the fire was
hardly noticed, if at all. Ha! ha! so far my plans have
worked admirably. Not one, even my own servant, noticed
my abscence from the house. Oh, Jacob! when they outdo
you in artifice they must be on the alert.

DRUCILLA (*enters* R. 3 E.). Well, Jacob, so you have
lost the mill. I expected as much when you turned Phillip
into the street. Do you know I look upon that act as an
abominable piece of rascality? (*Comes down* R. H. C.)

JACOB (L. C.). And why, please let me ask? Did I
overstep the limits of the law? Every man must look out for
his own interests regardless of his neighbor. As for the pe-
cuniary loss on the mill, that was nothing, for it was heavily
insured.

DRU. Well, I shall never overlook the way you have used
that family. Phillip, blind and almost helpless — just think
of it. It's a disgraceful reproach upon the name of Johnson.

JACOB (*irritated*). Look here, Drucilla, I'm not in the
right mood this morning to receive a curtain lecture. If you
can't come in here and talk with more civility, you had better remain without. (*Goes down* L. H. E.)

DRU. (*going down* C.). Indeed! indeed! Mr. Johnson.
Are you aware whom you are addressing? Remember, I am
your sister.

JACOB. Yes, and sometimes sisters can make themselves
disagreeable. I know my own business without any of your
interference. Of late you have seen fit to meddle with my
affairs more than is acceptable.

DRU. I want to know! Am I not the mistress of this
house? Who figures the interest on your notes, keeps your
books, gets your meals, and even darns your stockings?
Who, week in and week out, counsels me on business matters they are not capable of managing themselves? Mr.
Johnson, outside from bombast and cynicism, you are of but
little account. (*Returns* R. I E.)

JACOB (*seating himself at table* C. L.). Well, well, Drucilla, we won't quarrel. I am irritable this morning, I admit.
You are a good sister, and, if I do say it, full of excellent
qualities : but sometimes it does seem as if you talked a little
too much. However, I think I could hardly do without you.

DRU. Still you will insist upon getting another mistress, and as you are well aware, quite contrary to my wishes.

JACOB. That is a matter of an entirely different nature. Already I have the girl's consent. Even now I am expecting her, that we may arrange matters for the coming event.

DRU. Indeed! you had not informed me of this?

JACOB. I thought it was not necessary.

DRU. No; it is not necessary I should know anything. That girl, Mr. Johnson, will be a useless appendage. Am I not as good in my capacity, as a wife?

JACOB. Hardly, Drucilla.

DRU. Well, anyway, I know the girl does not marry you willingly. It is done to save her parents from the web you have woven around them; and for my part, I think it is an outrageous piece of business. (*Exit hurriedly* R. 3 E.)

JACOB. So, so, snarl like a lynx if you want to. If you knew the truth you might even growl. My mind is set upon winning that girl, and may I be cursed if I don't do it. (*Rises and goes down* C.) Where can that servant have betaken himself? I have not seen him this morning. Ah! I hear a step. He has either returned, or it is the girl I am expecting. (*Returns to table.* MABEL, *very pale, enters* C.) Ah! Miss Raymond. I have been awaiting your arrival. Please be seated. (*Offers chair.*)

MABEL (*down* R.). With your permission, I prefer standing. I have come here pursuant to your command. To plead with you, I know is useless. I now await your orders.

JACOB (*seating himself* C. L.). Miss Raymond, I had hoped to have found you more consistent; but if you continue to remain obstinate, it will be to your own detriment. Already I have suffered considerable loss at your father's hands; and the burning of the mill, which you have learned, no doubt, has made it even greater. Still, with your hand in marriage, I will overlook these losses, reinstate your parents in there old home, and even rebuild the mill.

MABEL. I understand. You would purchase me, body and soul, with money. You care not how many hearts you are breaking, or whether I love you or not, if only you can possess me. To save my parents, I come before you. If a merciful Heaven will hear my prayers, I shall be saved from this thraldom. If not, then with you I must submit to drag out my miserable existence.

JACOB. Am I to understand from this that my offer is accepted?

MABEL. Take it as you choose.

JACOB. Then I shall claim your hand. To consummate matters, I shall request that the wedding take place without delay. Your parents well established, and yourself surrounded with every luxury, I trust you will look upon your situation with a degree of happiness.

MABEL. Is the bird, taken from its native element and caged, ever happy? Does the galley slave, chained, to the oar, ever sense a thrill of joy? No more can I, caged, chained to a man I utterly loathe and despise, know what joy or happiness means.

JACOB. Well, if you will persist upon making yourself miserable, you alone must suffer. Sometime yon may think differently. (*Elias seen in archway.* JACOB *perceives him, and starts to his feet with a cry. Chord.*) Great Heavens!

ELIAS (*pale and haggard-looking*). I be no spirit, Jacob Johnson.

JACOB (*feebly*). You — you —

ELIAS. Oh! I ha' no doubt ye be surprised t' see me; but afore I ha' done with ye, ye will be more surprised. (*Advancing.*)

MABEL (*rushing to* ELIAS). Oh, Elias, my old friend, can you save me?

ELIAS. I be a working for ye, Mabel, I be a working for ye. First, tell me why ye ha' come t' this house?

MABEL. O Elias! I am here to save my parents. Only by marrying that man can it be accomplished. I have promised him my hand.

JACOB (*recovering himself*). And she shall keep her promise if the devil stands in the way.

ELIAS. Be not too sure, Jacob. I ha' made a covenant with myself t' protect her; and I be going t' do it, even unto death.

(*Noise without.* PHILLIP *heard speaking off* C. *All look toward* C.)

PHILLIP (*without*). Lead me into the house. Take me to wheer I can meet that man, and stand afore him face to face.

MABEL (*sinking into chair* R. H. C.). Oh, Heavens ! my father.

JACOB (*excitedly*). Curse him ! why is he here?

ELIAS (C. L.). He has come, Jacob, t' save his daughter.

LUCY (*speaking as she enters*). Land a massey! who'd a thought it.

(*Enter* C. MR. *and* MRS. RAYMOND *and* LUCY.)

MRS. R. Here we are, Phillip. The man you seek is before you.

PHILLIP (*standing* C. MRS. RAYMOND *to the right of him, and* LUCY *near* R. 3. E.). Then let me speak to him. Let me say to him as to how I pronounces him a villain. Tell him to return the daughter as he called from me, or may he live accursed of God.

MABEL (*going to him and putting her arms around his neck*). O father! I am here. Your Mabel is safe.

PHILLIP (*caressing her*). And is this my Mabel? My Mabel safe from the fangs of that viper, as he is? Tell me, my child, why you wounded my 'art by coming here.

MABEL. O father! I done it to save you. Only by my marrying that man can you be free.

PHILLIP. Then let me rot ! No child of mine are a-going through life bound to a man as devils would blush to own. Hunger shall come ; prison shall come ; death shall come, afore you shall wed that theer Jacob.

JACOB. Bah ! you are a lot of crazy fools. Don't think I will easily consent to yield after addressing to me such a homily. Beware, Phillip Raymond, or the prison shall receive you with all your infirmities.

PHILLIP. Theer are worse places for an honest man than a prison ; and one on 'em — I am arnest in saying it — is the standing in your presence. Already through your villainy, as I knows on, you have robbed me of everything but freedom. Take that, if as how you wants it, and the life wot goes with it; but this here child of mine, may God strike her dead afore she ever becomes your wife.

JACOB. If this is your answer, then have you sealed your own fate. Thwarted from wedlock with this girl, I will hurl you all down to the lowest depths it is possible for my nature to conceive. I tell you I am resolved and will triumph.

LUCY. Land a massey ! what a wretch.

MRS. R.   O Phillip! think upon your fate.

PHILLIP.   Out upon my fate, Betty, out upon it! The shark has bitten me afore, theerfore the second bite will come the more nat'ral to bear.   The worst he can do by me will not torture me half as much like as if his plan had succeeded. Bear a hand, Betty, and give me a seat.   I can stand no longer.   (*He is assisted to chair near* R. H. *corner.* MRS. RAYMOND *stands* R. *of him,* MABEL L., *and* LUCY *down* C. R.)   Theer, that will do.

ELIAS (*who has remained standing near* C. L., *now approaches table*).   If ye ha' a mind, Jacob, I would ask of ye a question.

JACOB.   Well!

ELIAS.   Ha' ye failed t' remember the warning I gave ye, or do ye look upon my words as of no account?

JACOB.   I look upon them as so much chaff.   What are you that I should have cause to fear?   (*Contemptuously.*) Nothing but a crack-brain and half idiot.

ELIAS (*wildly*).   What! ye call me idiot?   Ye dare t' say that I be an idiot?   Now shall ye tremble at my curse. Oh, I be mad — mad!   Five years ha' I cringed before ye like a slave, when ye should ha' been my slave, and crawled in the dust at my feet.   Oh, Jacob!   I ha' ye spread out before me where I can read ye like a book; and ye be all devil — devil.   (*Clasping his brow with his hands.*)   O Elias! what ha' ye t' live for now?   Now shall ye die, and show this fiend up t' the world.   (*Takes phial from his pocket.*

MABEL (*going towards him.*)   O Elias! what would you do?

ELIAS (*motioning her back*).   Go back, Mabel, go back. I would free ye, an' I ha' but one way t' do it.   Come not near me now.   (*Mabel goes back.*)   If ye love Edward, an' if ye love your parents. ye must listen t' my words, but make no attempt t' save me.

MABEL.   But you would do yourself harm?

ELIAS.   I be of no account.   My life ha' been a curse, an' there be one who ha' cursed it.   I be bound by an oath, an' the revealing of it can only be done on my dying day. This shall be that day, an' ye must not interfere.

JACOB (*in evident alarm*).   Elias, beware!   Do nothing rash or you will repent it.   (*Aside.*)   The first 'word he utters of that murder, I will stab him to the heart.

ELIAS. Hark ye, Jacob, t' my words. Ye thought to destroy your enemies when you burned the mill. Ye —

PHILLIP (*interrupting*). Wheer away, theer! wheer away. The mill — has that theer mill been burned? (*Attempts to rise. Is held back by* MRS. RAYMOND *and* MABEL.)

LUCY. Well, now, I ain't a bit surprised.

ELIAS. Ye listen t' my words, Phillip, an' ye will find out.

PHILLIP. But I want to know if that theer mill has been burned?

MABEL. It has, dear father, it burned last night.

PHILLIP. Oh curse him! curse — (*Mrs.* RAYMOND *and* LUCY *quiet him as* ELIAS *continues.*)

ELIAS. I ha' told ye, Jacob, that ye thought t' destroy us by burning the mill; but I ha' escaped, for which I ha' your confederate t' thank. Now, Jacob, I be going t' make you tremble.

JACOB (*savagely*). Do it at your peril. Beware! you never shall live to utter a syllable. (*Starts to draw knife.*)

ELIAS. Jacob I ha' come prepared. (*Suddenly draws revolver, and points it at* JACOB *across table. Chord.* JACOB *staggers back and sinks into chair.*) Now ye move afore I ha' finished, an' ye shall die along with me.

JACOB. But you do not mean —

ELIAS. I do mean that I be going t' die; an' my last words will be the revealing of that oath. Now I want ye all t' listen; but let no one, not even my friends, interfere with me, or it will be at their peril.

(*Music.* ELIAS *stands* C. *with revolver pointed at* JACOB. *All look at him as if stupefied. In his left hand is the phial. He removes cork, slowly raises bottle and is about to drink, when shouts are heard without. He pauses a moment, during which,* EDWARD *followed by* SAMBO, *rush into the room from* C., EDWARD *shouting " Saved! saved!" as he enters.*)

EDWARD (*down* C.). Kill the fatted calf, for the prodigal has returned. Mabel, I'm a free man. I've got back that money from the man who stole it.

MABEL (*throwing herself into his arms*). Heaven be praised! Now is Elias saved from his terrible doom.

ELIAS (*who has lowered revolver and stands* C. L.). The money has nothing t' do with the oath. I be going t' die an' reveal that.

EDW. Well, now, I reckon you won't. Say! Elias, the cat's out of the bag. I've got the whole sum and substance of that oath down on this paper. Here it is. (*Takes paper from his pocket.*)

JACOB (*starting toward him*). Curse you! give me that paper.

ELIAS (*starting forward and pointing revolver at* JACOB). Ye go back!

JACOB (*retreating; aside*). My game is up.

ELIAS. Edward, will ye speak those words again? I ha' a fear that I did not understand. What was it ye said about the oath?

EDW. I said I knew the whole sum and substance of it; and I've got the proof to back it up. The murder that was committed here five years ago was done by Jacob Johnson.

MABEL (*clinging to* EDWARD). O Heavens!

LUCY. Land a massey!

JACOB. You lie! The man who informed you has done it to clear himself.

EDW. The proof is in black and white on this paper, with your name to back it.

JACOB (*aside*). I am a doomed man.

PHILLIP. I warn't no better opinion of the man then to believe it. He led me into a forgery of his own making, and the man as would do that, would murder.

MRS. R. O Phillip! what an escape our Mabel has had.

ELIAS. Well, Jacob, what ha' ye t' say t' the charge that is laid against ye.

JACOB (*despairingly*). I have nothing to say. Tell me, if you will, the whereabouts of the man who has made this disclosure?

EDW. He is dead. His dying words was the confession to that crime. Evil though he was, he couldn't hold a candle to you, if I do say it.

JACOB. Save your taunts, young man, they are useless. As the Fates have conspired against me, I may as well hasten my doom. In yonder cabinet are the papers bearing Phillip's signature. The forgery he committed was concocted by

myself. It was I who arranged the papers for him to sign.
You can destroy them. I suppose you have no objection to
my visiting my sister; There are some matters I wish to
arrange. (*Starts off.*)

EDW. (*stopping him*). Wait, Jacob, you need a conductor. (*Calling off.*) Here, officer, you are wanted! (*Enter
officer* C.) This man is in want of bracelets. Put them on
and lead him to his sister. Let him escape at your peril.

OFFICER. Mr. Johnson, you are my prisoner.

JACOB. Umph! there is no need mentioning that. (*He
is handcuffed. Starts off.*) All together, you have con-
quered. That you may be cursed, though, with all the
tortures of an Ixion, is my parting blessing. (*Exit with
officer,* R. 3 E.)

SAMBO (*who has remained near* R. C.). Good-bye, Mas'r
Johnson. Golly! but dis yer chile had a narrow escape, I
kin tole yer.

LUCY. Land sakes! you don't s'pose he would touch a
nigger, du ye?

PHILLIP. Theer is more evil in that theer Jacob than in
old Satan himself.

EDW. And he took it all with him when he went out.
(*Crossing to* ELIAS *with* MABEL.) Elias, my old friend,
why are you so silent?

ELIAS (*down* C. EDWARD *and* MABEL *to* R. *of him*). I
be dumb, Edward, I be dumb. I ha' not the power t'
express the thoughts that be raging here. (*Places hand
upon his heart.*) T' be free from that accursed oath — oh,
it be Heaven itself! But I can't realize it, Edward, I can't
realize it.

MABEL. You will in time, Elias, and then we all shall be
so happy.

EDW. You just bet we shall. You can take that money
and invest it in stocks. We shant want it; or — er — I
mean, Phillip won't. As for myself, I got the grand bounce
at home, and I suppose I shall here — eh, Mabel?

MABEL. Not so long as that dollar lasts, and you behave
yourself.

PHILLIP. Well, Edward, if you loves this here child of
mine, as I loves her, you can have her. I will re-build the
mill with Elias for a partner. Being as now I am useless

myself, you shall take my place. (*Lifting his hands.*)
Theer, children, now may God bless you.

Mrs. R.   And make you as happy as I am at the present
moment.

Lucy.   Land a massey! Uriah used tu say that the only
happiness he ever knew, wus settin' down tu a good dinner.
Gracious! that makes me think of that fricerseed chicken.

Sambo.   Lor a mighty! took us to it.

Edw.   Yes, let us go. I want to get out of here as soon
as possible. What say you, Elias?

Elias.   I be ready, Edward, I be ready. The good Lord
has answered my prayers, an' I would bless him for it; but I
ha' not the mind t' do it here. If there be happiness in store
for me, I be thankful for it; but never — never, if I live the
life of the oldest, oh never again let me be BOUND BY AN
OATH.

(*Disposition of characters.*)

SAMBO.

LUCY.   ELIAS.

PHILLIP.   EDWARD.

MRS. RAYMOND.   MABEL.

R.   L.

CURTAIN.

www.ingramcontent.com/pod-product-compliance
Lightning Source LLC
Chambersburg PA
CBHW030000030726
47499CB00008B/2831